Ex Libris

"I wish I'd never
set eyes on you!"

Tammy gasped and stared at Hugo, her green eyes wide with distress. "You really know how to make a girl feel uncomfortable, don't you? How do you think I feel knowing I'm only here on sufferance?"

"I don't care how you feel," he rasped. "I just wish to God you weren't here now."

How cruel he was! Tammy felt a cold shiver run down her spine. "You have only yourself to blame," she said coldly.

What Tammy couldn't understand was that if Hugo was so much against her being on his boat, why didn't he do something about it? After all, she was totally in his hands. Until Hugo contacted Emil Conin about her stolen things, she was his prisoner. It was as simple as that.

Harlequin Premiere Editions

Harlequin Premiere Editions

PIRATE LOVER

Margaret Mayo

Harlequin Books

TORONTO • LONDON • LOS ANGELES • AMSTERDAM
SYDNEY • HAMBURG • PARIS • STOCKHOLM • ATHENS • TOKYO

Original hardcover edition published in 1980
by Mills & Boon Limited

ISBN 0-373-82111-5

This Harlequin Premiere Editions volume
published October 1981

Copyright© 1980 by Margaret Mayo.
Philippine copyright 1980. Australian copyright 1980.
All rights reserved. Except for use in any review, the reproduction or
utilization of this work in whole or in part in any form by any electronic,
mechanical or other means, now known or hereafter invented, including
xerography, photocopying and recording, or in any information storage or
retrieval system, is forbidden without the permission of the publisher,
Harlequin Enterprises Limited, 225 Duncan Mill Road, Don Mills, Ontario,
Canada M3B 3K9. All the characters in this book have no existence outside
the imagination of the author and have no relation whatsoever to anyone
bearing the same name or names. They are not even distantly inspired by
any individual known or unknown to the author, and all the incidents are
pure invention.
The Harlequin trademark, consisting of the words HARLEQUIN PREMIERE
EDITIONS and the portrayal of a Harlequin, is registered in the United
States Patent Office and in the Canada Trade Marks Office.

Printed in U.S.A.

CHAPTER ONE

For the first time Tammy regretted the impulse which had made her take this holiday alone. Until a few hours ago she had found the whole adventure exciting, a new experience, now her mind was filled with doubt plus a certain amount of fear.

If David had not been so dedicated to his career this would have been their honeymoon and she would not have found herself in the unfortunate position of having to share a villa with a strange Frenchman and his wife. Admittedly Pierre and Simone were friends of David's, but that did not excuse Pierre for making amorous advances the moment they were alone.

When she had arrived at the villa earlier that day the Pascals had been shocked to see her alone and to learn that the wedding had been postponed because David had flown to the other side of the world to try and capture an export order, which would make several millions for the engineering company of which he was sales director.

Tammy had never resented him putting his job first, until now. She had in fact secretly admired the ambition which had taken him up to his present position at the age of twenty-five. But when it had interfered with their wedding arrangements she had had a blazing row and horrified David by declaring that she was going to France alone. He was not going to do her out of a holiday even if he was depriving her of becoming Mrs David Gordon.

When the Pascals heard of her plight they had insisted on staying on at the villa to look after her and Tammy had been delighted to accept—until Simone had gone shopping and Pierre had shown signs of becoming too friendly.

Now, in the sanctity of her room, her heart still beating rapidly following the tussle with Pierre on the settee, she tried to decide what to do. She could not stay here, that was for certain, but where could she go in this foreign country where she did not even know the language?

When she heard the front door close Tammy looked through the window and saw Pierre climb into his car and drive away. She breathed an unconscious sigh of relief and without giving herself time to think picked up her suitcase, which she had fortunately not yet unpacked, and let herself out of the house, leaving a short note for Simone apologising for any inconvenience but declaring that she had decided against holidaying alone after all. With luck they would think she had returned to England and that would be the last she would see of the French Romeo.

Once in the street she hailed a taxi which took her into the heart of Nice and entered the first hotel she came to. She had not stopped to consider that it was the height of the season and was appalled when she was told there were no rooms available either here or in any other hotel in the town.

Disappointed, and resigning herself to the fact that she might have to return to England after all, Tammy made her way to the bar and ordered a Pernod, despite the fact that it was only three-thirty in the afternoon.

Sitting alone at a table, she scarcely registered the fact that someone had taken the seat next to hers, and it was not until a male voice with a strong French accent addressed her that she looked up from the glass she had been twirling absently through her fingers.

Her wide green eyes stared hostilely at the stranger, noticing automatically his dark good looks and the intimate manner in which he was regarding her. Were all Frenchmen potential Don Juans? she wondered hopelessly, preparing herself for the fact that she might have to make yet another hasty exit.

'*Pardon, mademoiselle*, I could not help overhearing that you were looking for a room. Perhaps I can help? Emil is the name, Emil Conin.'

Tammy treated him to a disdainful glare. 'I don't think so,' she returned coldly, and raising her glass she drank the liquid quickly and stood up. '*Au revoir*, Monsieur Conin.' She lifted her chin determinedly and stalked from the room, aware that many pairs of eyes followed her exit with undisguised admiration.

She was a pretty girl, not very tall, but with fiery red hair and a temper to match which made up for anything she might lack in height. Her face was heart-shaped and her generous mouth smiled as easily as it pouted. At the moment, though, she was far from happy, and when Emil Conin followed her outside she rounded on him hotly, her green eyes blazing and her slender body stiff with anger.

'Are you following me, *monsieur*? If so, you're wasting your time. I'm about to catch a plane back to England.' Her mind had been suddenly made up when she realised how vulnerable a girl alone in France could be.

He shrugged in a typical Gallic gesture. 'I think you're being very foolish. At least listen to my proposition—you might be pleasantly surprised.'

Tammy reluctantly conceded that it could do no harm and dropping her heavy suitcase to the floor she placed her handbag on top of it and faced him impatiently. 'Okay, what is this marvellous offer you're so sure I won't be able to resist?'

He smiled mysteriously. 'You're very attractive, *ma chérie*, exactly the type of girl I am looking for.'

'For what purpose?' Tammy shot him a look of horror, unable to voice the thoughts that had immediately entered her mind.

'I need a croupier—for my night club,' came the swift, cool reply. 'If you take the job there's a furnished apartment thrown in.'

'Sharing with you, I suppose?' she threw back furiously. 'What type of girl do you take me for? Besides, I'm not looking for work, I'm here on holiday.'

Unperturbed, he smiled. 'You would have your days free to do whatever you like. The work is during the evenings only. You would be a fool to turn down my offer. The money is very high and you would still be getting your holiday.'

'I'm afraid it doesn't appeal to me,' she said tightly, bending down to retrieve her luggage. 'I'm sorry, Mon——' Her words were cut off in mid-sentence. 'My handbag, it's gone!' She glared at him accusingly. 'Where is it?'

He spread his hands expansively. 'You may search me if you wish, but I can assure you that you won't find your bag on my person.'

'I'm not expecting to,' Tammy cried, 'but it was your idea, wasn't it? Keeping me talking while someone else steals my bag, and then with no money and no passport I'll be obliged to take your crummy job!'

'You exaggerate, *mademoiselle*. I would do no such thing.'

'No? You could have fooled me, but if you're not involved then you'll have no objection to directing me to the nearest police station?'

'I'll do better than that,' he said calmly, 'I'll take you. My car is just around the corner. Here, let me take your case.' Before Tammy could stop him he had picked up the brown leather holdall and was leading the way to his car.

She had no alternative but to follow, but she did so reluctantly, studying his back with mutinous anger, determined to voice her suspicions to the police.

The building he took her to looked nothing like the police stations in England, but appreciating that here they might be different, she followed him unquestioningly inside. It was not until he took her into an expensively furnished room that Tammy realised she had been tricked.

After casting one scornful look at the white fur rugs and mirrored walls she swung round intending to leave, only to find that Emil Conin had locked the door and was facing her with an infuriating grin.

'You would not listen,' he said apologetically, 'so I was compelled to take matters into my own hands. You will enjoy the work, I know, and you will be free to come and go as you like, as soon as you give me your word that you will not try to run away.'

Tammy stamped one delicate foot angrily. 'You

—you low-down, lying hypocrite! You haven't heard the last of this, I assure you,' and she folded her arms, staring at him defiantly.

Almost as though she hadn't spoken Emil crossed the room to a drinks cabinet and poured her a Pernod. 'Your favourite drink, I imagine?' passing it to her with a bland smile.

She took the glass and swallowed the liquid eagerly, not because she wanted the drink but to give her courage to get through the next few hours. If she read him correctly Emil would not let her out of his sight, so for the time being it might pay to pretend to defer to his wishes.

He could not keep her guarded every second, though, and as soon as the opportunity presented itself she would escape and find her way to the nearest police station.

She dropped into the nearest chair. 'Okay, you win. What is it you want me to do? I ought to warn you, perhaps, that I know nothing about gambling and speak no French.'

'No matter.' His easy smile made her almost believe that his offer of help had been genuine. If her bag hadn't gone missing she might have, as it was mistrust was uppermost in her mind.

He flung open a wardrobe to reveal a glittering array of seductive evening dresses. 'These are your work clothes. They won't all be in your size, but I'm sure you'll find something suitable. I want you to wear one tonight. You'll be with Suzanne, she'll show you what to do, so watch her closely, because tomorrow you'll be on your own.'

He left the room, the door closing with an

ominous click so that without even trying it Tammy knew it was locked.

She viewed the dresses with distaste but resigned to the fact that she would have to wear something if she was to carry this farce through she selected one, and threw it on to the bed before shutting herself in the adjoining bathroom.

It was sumptuous in the extreme and relaxing in a hot scented bath she could almost forget what had happened and pretend that she was staying in some exclusive hotel and enjoying the holiday of a lifetime.

A meal was brought to her on a tray, but it was not until Emil put in an appearance a few hours later that the enormous reality of the situation struck her.

She had already slipped into the emerald velvet gown which was the least suggestive of the dresses, but even so she felt exposed. The colour suited her and matched her vivid green eyes, but as far as Tammy was concerned it was all a part of this charade she was being forced to enact.

David would have a fit if he saw her. He was so conservative, making no pretence of the fact that he was attracted to her because she was a nice sensible girl with modest tastes. The thought of his outraged expression if he should see her in this get-up made her laugh.

'Ah, that is better,' said Emil at once. 'I was beginning to get worried that you would not look happy tonight, and that would have been bad for business, don't you agree?'

Tammy shrugged, her smile quickly fading at this reminder of what was in store. 'I couldn't care less.

I'm only obliging because I have no alternative.'

His quick frown frightened her and she turned away, making a pretence of brushing out her shoulder-length hair.

Her heart was pumping at twice its normal rate as she studied his reflection through the mirror. His back was turned to her, but there was a ruthlessness about him that made her all the more determined to find some way of escaping.

The casino was not far away, but even so it was impossible to remember every turn he took and she knew that it would be impossible to find her way back herself. There went the remotest chance of recovering her suitcase.

Suzanne was a pretty dark-eyed French girl who greeted Tammy with a polite but distant smile and made it appear that she was doing the English girl a great favour by showing her exactly what she was expected to do.

The room soon became full of people and Tammy found her attention more on a means of escape than how the game was played. Several times she found Emil's watchful eyes upon her and had to force her attention back to the bright green baize cloth with its red, black and gold lines and lettering. The roulette wheel mesmerised her as the ivory ball clicked round with each spin.

There were three croupiers to this particular game, one to spin the wheel and the others to collect and pay the bets at each end of the table. Soon the excitement and glamour of the occasion had Tammy mesmerised and she forgot all about trying to get away as she watched the happy faces of the players as they won, or disappointment when they had placed a high bet and lost.

One man in particular took her attention. He was not playing, merely watching, but several times their eyes met, his dark and smouldering and disapproving. Try as she might Tammy could not ignore him even though there was cruel condescension on that arrogant face.

His dinner jacket sat easily on wide powerful shoulders, his black hair almost reached his collar. Full lips were compressed tightly together as yet again he allowed his eyes to watch her in open contemplation.

She judged him to be in his early thirties and for a few moments allowed herself to hold his gaze, noting the high noble brow, his lean, slightly elongated face, a crooked nose that looked at one time as though it might have been broken. He was a good few inches taller than the rest of the company and had an air of authority about him that made her wonder who he might be.

Suzanne, shaking her arm impatiently, drew Tammy back to the table and she was forced to forget the man opposite, concentrating all her attention on the rules of the game. Only when the game was over and the players were placing their bets ready for the next one did she allow her eyes to flicker yet again in his direction.

He had gone—and she did not know whether to feel disappointed or pleased, but when a firm hand touched her elbow, pulling her away from the table, she knew instinctively that it was him and just as automatically struggled. It was only when her eyes caught Emil's, who was nodding firmly as much as to say that being nice to customers was part of her duty, that she ceased.

The stranger led her away from the table to a

corner of the room where the crowds were not so dense. 'You're new here,' he stated categorically in English. 'You're not the type Conin usually employs. Are you sure you know exactly what it is you've let yourself in for?'

Tammy stared at him haughtily, noting at closer quarters the silver which streaked his hair. 'What I do is no concern of yours.'

'True,' he admitted seriously, 'but I don't like to see a fellow Englander being taken for a ride, that's why I wished to speak to you, to ask if you——' He broke off, shrugging. 'Conin's girls have quite a reputation.'

What he was insinuating frightened Tammy, even though it was no more than she had thought herself, but she was even more annoyed that this man should see fit to interfere. For the moment she forgot about trying to run away, even the fact that this man could be of help. 'I don't believe you,' she cried rashly. 'My job is a croupier, nothing else.'

'And for that you get a free apartment and a very generous salary?'

She nodded, feeling her anger begin to diminish and a horrifying feeling that he was speaking the truth.

'What kind of a fool are you?' he rasped harshly. 'Conin doesn't give anything away for nothing. How did you come to get mixed up in this racket?'

Tammy lifted her shoulders helplessly. 'He overheard me trying to get a room at the Ambassador and he offered to help. Then my handbag was stolen, so I didn't have much choice.'

The stranger raised his eyes skywards. 'You gullible little fool! Conin will have your bag, it's one of his favourite tricks. You'd better get out of here before anything else happens to you.'

'Like this?' asked Tammy, her face pale now as the full potential of her situation struck her.

'I'll take you to your apartment to pick up the rest of your stuff.' He caught her arm in a vice-like grip and half dragged her across the room.

She glanced across at Emil, but he was smiling approvingly, no doubt believing that she was giving the service he intended.

Outside last-minute doubts assailed Tammy and she refused to get into the stranger's car. 'How do I know you're speaking the truth?' she cried. 'How do I know it's you, not Emil Conin, I can trust?'

'You'll just have to take my word for it,' he said grimly.

Tammy was in a dilemma. Emil had appeared kind on the surface, it was only this man who had put doubts into her mind. How did she know that he had not some ulterior motive in rushing her away from the casino?

'You'd better make up your mind quickly,' he said at length, holding the door open, his long fingers strumming impatiently on top.

But when she thought of Emil's face, his approval when he saw her going out of the room with this man, she knew he must be speaking the truth. Otherwise Emil would surely have stopped her.

With a resigned sigh she climbed into the car. The deep leather seats were conductive to relaxing, but she sat upright, nervously twisting David's ring on her finger.

'What's the address?' asked the dark man shortly, as he slid in beside her.

It was then that Tammy had to admit that she had not the slightest idea.

He shook his head in total exasperation, clearly considering her all kinds of a fool. His eyes flickered towards the ring. 'What's your fiancé thinking, letting you travel alone when you're obviously incapable of looking after yourself?'

'What business is it of yours?' parried Tammy hostilely.

'You certainly need someone to look after you and until you get your handbag, and presumably your passport, back I think you'd better come along with me.'

Tammy felt that she was spending her entire holiday fleeing from the unwanted attentions of various members of the opposite sex and knew that she could fight no more. He seemed genuine enough, on the surface, and at least he was English, that was something in his favour.

Sinking tiredly into her seat, she nodded, 'I don't seem to have much choice,' and she closed her eyes. She was conscious of the busy sounds of night life in Nice, but after a few miles the laughter and music faded. Looking about her she discovered that they were driving along a road which ran fairly close to the sea, with cliffs rising high on the other side.

Her companion remained silent and she felt too drowsy to question him about their destination, closing her eyes again and very soon falling into a deep dreamless sleep.

CHAPTER TWO

When Tammy woke it was morning and she could not at first recall what had happened. Aware only that she was in a strange bed she lay for a few moments trying to recollect her thoughts.

She was warm and comfortable, but uneasy, and when her eyes alighted on the green velvet dress lying across the bottom of her bed memories came flooding back and she shot up, mortified to find herself naked and drawing the sheets quickly about her.

Her eyes darted anxiously about the room. It was square and small, though pleasantly furnished, and the window was round, reminding her of a porthole.

Trying to push to the back of her mind that someone must have undressed her last night, she scrambled out of bed, wrapping the sheet about her sari-style, and padded across to the window. To her amazement it *was* a porthole, and she looked out across a narrow strip of water to the shining white side of another ship anchored alongside them.

Determined now to find out exactly what had happened to her, and not altogether sure that she had not been kidnapped, Tammy tried the cabin door, only to find, as she had suspected, that it was locked. Another door revealed a toilet and bathroom, tempting her to freshen herself up before meeting whatever the day had to offer.

She dropped the sheet to the floor at the same time as her cabin door opened. She screamed and dragged it about her again quickly, staring hostilely at the dark man who seemed amused by her heightened colour.

'The least you could have done was knocked!' she flared angrily.

'I thought you might still be asleep and I didn't want to wake you,' he said blandly. 'I apologise if my presence embarrasses you. Perhaps you might feel easier if you knew that this was not the first time I've seen you naked.'

'It was you who undressed me?' Tammy felt almost faint with shame and humiliation. 'You've got a cheek,' her temper now beginning to supersede all other feelings. 'Why didn't you wake me? There was no need for that, none at all.'

She was absolutely mortified that this man, a total stranger, should have taken it upon himself to divest her of her clothing. It made her wonder what else he had done, and she couldn't imagine how she could have slept through it all. Though she had risen early yesterday morning and done a fair amount of travelling—it could account for the fact that she had gone out like a light.

'Your honour's still intact, if that's what's worrying you,' he said with an irritating smile. 'If you like, I'll come back in ten minutes when you're dressed.'

'I'd prefer to talk now,' said Tammy tightly, sitting down on the edge of the bed and drawing the sheet closer. 'I want to know where I am and what you're going to do with me.'

He laughed and advanced further into the room. Tammy backed on to the bed, pressing herself against the wall, not altogether trusting this handsome stranger who had the advantage of having seen her at her most vulnerable.

'I won't hurt you,' he said shortly.

'Then why did you lock me in?' she shot back.

'Because,' he explained impatiently, 'I didn't want you running away and involving yourself in more trouble. You strike me as being impulsive, and there are a few characters around here who wouldn't be averse to taking advantage of a pretty young girl who's all alone.'

'I'm not so young,' she retorted indignantly. 'I'm twenty-one, quite old enough to know what I'm doing. I suppose you're trying to tell me that you're not like that?' She eyed him steadily, unable to understand why he should be going to all this trouble on her behalf unless he had an ulterior motive.

'If I was, would I have rescued you from Emil Conin's clutches? Wouldn't I have taken advantage of the situation there and then?'

'I don't know,' shrugged Tammy helplessly. 'This whole holiday's turning into a nightmare—I wish I'd never decided to come.'

'An impulsive decision?' he queried, and tilting his head to one side added consideringly, 'Let me see, I suspect you had a row with the boy-friend, otherwise you'd have been here together?'

'On honeymoon,' muttered Tammy beneath her breath, not really intending him to hear, but he did and lifted his brows enquiringly. 'We didn't argue,' she defended hotly. 'His business took him to New Zealand. We had to postpone the wedding, that's all, but I didn't see why we should forfeit the money we'd already paid, so I came along.' She finished with a defiant shrug, daring him to question her further.

He frowned strongly as though the situation puzzled him. 'If your holiday was already booked why were you trying to find rooms? It doesn't make sense.'

'Well——' Tammy hesitated, and then decided she might as well tell him the whole story. He would wheedle it out of her one way or another if he really wanted to, he seemed that sort. 'We'd arranged to rent the villa of a friend of David's, but I didn't like Pierre.'

'Why?' he asked abruptly, 'or shall I hazard a guess? He too was tempted to take advantage? There's something about you that tempts a man, do you know that? I'm really surprised that—David, did you say his name was? let you loose alone. I wouldn't if you were mine.'

'Since I'm not,' snapped Tammy, 'I'll thank you to keep your nose out of my business. Perhaps, Mr Whatever-your-name-is, you'll kindly tell me where we are and what plans you have in mind so far as I'm concerned?'

'The name's Kane, Hugo Kane,' and his dark eyes, thickly fringed with black lashes, studied her with an insolent disregard for her feelings, 'and you're in Monte Carlo harbour aboard the *Flying Queen*, one of a fleet of the finest yachts you'll find anywhere in the world.' He sounded inordinately proud. 'As for what I'm going to do with you, I suggest you stay here and earn your keep until I manage to persuade Conin to hand over your property.'

Tammy eyed him warily. 'Earn my keep? What was it you had in mind?' Not surprisingly she could not help wondering whether his proposition ran along the same lines as Emil's.

'We're short of a crew member,' he said off-handedly. 'She went down sick at the last minute and it crossed my mind that you could be just the sort of person we're looking for.'

'I don't know anything about boats,' put in Tammy hastily.

'You don't need to. We need someone to keep it clean, do a bit of waitressing, generally making herself useful, you know the sort of thing?'

'No, I don't,' said Tammy distantly. 'If it's a cleaner you're after it's not exactly my line. Do I look like one?'

'If you did I wouldn't be asking you,' he said, lifting an eyebrow drily. 'We don't employ the usual sort of charlady, we like someone decorative.' He eyed her bared shoulders, coolly appraising the cleavage revealed by the slipping sheet. 'You fit the bill admirably.'

Tammy hitched the white cotton higher, her green eyes blazing furiously. 'What sort of a boat is this?' she asked suspiciously, not sure that she liked the sound of things.

'A holiday yacht,' he replied easily. 'Usually chartered during the season. You'd be a fool to turn down my proposition, this is easily the most luxurious yacht in the harbour, even though I say it my-self. Didn't you know that Monte Carlo is the world's most exclusive port?'

Tammy shrugged. 'Not really, but then I'm never likely to be in a position to be able to charter such a boat, so it wouldn't interest me. In fact I don't like boats very much. Do you own this one, or are you the captain—or are you perhaps chartering it?'

'It's mine,' he said succinctly, making it clear that

he did not want to discuss the matter further. 'Do I take it that the job doesn't appeal to you?'

Tammy realised that if she turned the offer down she would be losing the chance of a lifetime. Despite the work it would be interesting, and until she recovered her passport it would afford her a roof over her head.

'It does tempt me,' she admitted at last.

'But you're concerned with the proprieties of the situation?' he scoffed. 'You needn't be. The crew are a good crowd and my guests are both happily married couples.'

'How about you?' asked Tammy impudently. 'Are you married?'

A brief smile curved his lips. 'Not yet, but my fiancée is very possessive. She won't let me stray, so you need have no fears that I might——'

'I wasn't suggesting that,' interceded Tammy hotly, indignant that he should think that she thought him in any way interested in her. Surprisingly, though, she was a teeny bit disappointed that he was engaged. He was after all a very attractive man, one who would turn any woman's head.

A moment later she chided herself for entertaining such disloyal thoughts. She loved David and if it hadn't been for his dedication to his job they would have been married by now and none of this would have happened.

'Of course not,' he said solemnly. 'Now tell me what your name is, and while you're showering I'll see about finding you something to wear. You're much the same size as Andrea and she has so many clothes I'm sure she can spare some.'

'Tamsin Swift,' supplied Tammy readily, not at

all sure that she liked the idea of wearing another
woman's clothes, but seeing no alternative unless
she went around in that green thing. 'But my friends
call me Tammy.'

'Then Tammy it will be,' he said. 'I'll be back in
ten minutes.'

For a few seconds Tammy stared after him. He
was certainly some man, and shivers ran down her
spine at the sheer masculinity of him. This morning
he wore polished cotton slacks and a thin mesh shirt
which hid none of his muscular powerful chest.
There was something dangerous about him, a compelling magnetism that made her want to leave the
boat now.

Her heart beat fast and furious as she slid from the
bed, making her wonder why a stranger should
arouse these emotive feelings when all she had ever
felt for David was a warm glow.

There was some consolation in the fact that Hugo
Kane already had a girl; at least it meant that he
would spare no time for her. It could prove fatal if
he did. If she felt weak-limbed when he spoke to her,
what would happen if he made a pass? It didn't
bear thinking about, and determinedly she pushed
these thoughts to the back of her mind, throwing the
sheet on to the bed and stepping inside the shower
cubicle.

A cold shower soon rationalised her thoughts and
as she waited for Hugo to return she was able to
laugh at her fantasies, reminding herself that David
was her man and that as soon as he returned from
New Zealand they would be married.

Surprisingly the thought depressed her, but
rather than believe Hugo Kane had anything to do

with it she told herself firmly it was because this holiday had turned into a fiasco. Anyone would feel downhearted if they'd had her bad luck, she decided, but it was funny how her spirits lifted when Hugo returned.

'I'm afraid Andrea was not as obliging as I expected,' he said, and he seemed annoyed. 'But these should see you through for the moment. I'll take you into Monte Carlo later and you can get what you need.'

Before Tammy could object he had disappeared again. She herself was not surprised that the unknown Andrea had protested against lending her clothes to a stranger, but she was against the idea of Hugo Kane spending money on her. He had done her one favour already, he had no need to involve himself further. She would tell him as much the next time she saw him.

The scarlet trousers were a perfect fit, but the red and white striped top was cut daringly low and the colour really did nothing for her. Tammy wondered whether Hugo Kane had told his fiancée that she had auburn hair and that she had purposely chosen this colour knowing that in all probability it would not suit her.

It was a bitchy thought, she knew, but somehow she had the impression that Andrea was a bitchy person, and there and then made up her mind that she did not like her.

With a brush she found lying on the dressing table Tammy brushed her hair thoroughly, allowing its thick wavy length to fall about her shoulders. It did not matter that she had no make-up because she had a naturally healthy colour and long dark lashes which framed her beautiful eyes.

Indeed she was a striking girl, and when she let herself out of the cabin, now left unlocked, she tilted her chin mutinously, determined to make the best of this unfortunate situation.

The corridor was deserted, but at the end were steps leading upwards into another corridor, carpeted this time in a rich deep red. Several oak-panelled doors were all tightly closed, so she made her way up yet again.

Had Tammy not known that she was on a boat she would never have guessed it. The rooms that confronted her now were like nothing she had ever seen before. First of all there was a lounge, with an open fireplace at one end—filled at the moment with a beautiful display of fresh flowers—capable of taking a coal fire should the weather demand it. The walls were panelled in a rich red wood and several easy chairs and a settee in black leather were placed strategically about the thickly carpeted floor.

She passed through into yet another room, one end of which was divided into a dining area, with a long, highly-polished table, capable of seating up to twelve people.

At the moment everywhere was deserted and Tammy carried on with her explorations, finding a library, a hairdressing salon, and finally the kitchen which was better equipped than any house, let alone a boat, and she stood for a moment looking at the gleaming stainless steel and white formica.

When a footstep sounded behind her she turned, encountering the round face of a short stocky man in a white overall. 'Ah,' he said at once, 'you are the young lady who has come to take the place of Miss

Harriet. Hugo said I would not mistake your red hair.'

If there was anything Tammy hated it was her hair being described as red, but it was not this man's fault, so she showed none of her annoyance, instead smiling a greeting. 'I was admiring your kitchen. It must be a pleasure to work in.'

'It is indeed,' he said, holding out his hand. 'Let me introduce myself. I'm the chef, Ronald Chipman, commonly known as Chips. Welcome aboard the *Flying Queen*. I hope you'll be very happy with us. Have you met the rest of the crew yet?'

Tammy shook her head.

'They're not a bad lot,' he continued, 'but you'll have to watch Eddie Marchant, the chief steward, he's very fond of the ladies. There's no harm in him, though, and you look as if you're capable of looking after yourself.'

'I'm learning fast,' thought Tammy drily, but she liked this man, feeling instinctively that he was someone she could trust. 'I'm Tamsin Swift,' she said, 'but please call me Tammy, everyone does.'

'Tammy? I like it,' said a new voice, as an arm encircled her waist, twirling her round so that her eyes met a pair of smiling brown ones, and even white teeth flashed in an engaging grin. This, she presumed, was the incorrigible Eddie Marchant.

She wriggled free and treated him to a disdainful stare, determined to put him in his place from the start and let him see that she would stand no nonsense. 'The chief steward, I presume?' she said coolly.

'I see my reputation has preceded me,' he laughed, glancing accusingly at Chips. 'Take no notice of what he says. Any problems, come to me, I'll see you all right.'

'I bet you will,' she replied, but she could not help smiling. He had an easy outgoing nature that made him a likeable fellow. 'Perhaps you can start by telling me exactly what my duties are? Mr Kane told me briefly, but I'm not entirely sure what I'm expected to do.'

Eddie grinned and put his arm about her shoulders. 'Of course, my darling, come with me. Uncle Eddie will explain all.'

They were laughing together as they left the kitchen and Tammy looked back over her shoulder, pulling a helpless face at the smiling Chips. Consequently she did not see Hugo Kane approaching and the first she knew of his presence was when his deep voice boomed, 'That will do, Marchant. I'll explain to Miss Swift myself.'

The chief steward's arm dropped away with surprising speed and there was a sheepish look on his face as he walked away, making Tammy guess that this was not the first time Hugo had had to reprimand him for being too familiar.

'I'm sorry about that,' he said stiffly, as soon as Eddie was out of hearing. 'That young man's a nuisance where women are concerned, I ought to have warned you. But he's good at his job and I'd be reluctant to get rid of him.'

'He wasn't bothering me,' declared Tammy lightly. 'In fact, I found him rather charming.' Why she felt tempted to defend Eddie she did not know. He was nice, but that was all. He had none of Hugo Kane's fatal magnetism. Even now she felt the hairs on her spine prickling at his presence and an unaccustomed breathlessness making her voice slightly husky.

He frowned darkly down, his clear brown eyes hard and full of censure. 'Looks like I was mistaken as to the type of girl you are. Let me tell you now, I expect no fun and games among the crew. You work together as a team and you're good friends, but that is as far as it goes. Do I make myself clear?'

What else could she do but agree? She shrugged and said reluctantly, 'I suppose so,' and then on a more defensive note, 'but in my own time, I shan't expect you to dictate to me then.'

'What own time?' he asked loudly. 'Running this boat is a twenty-four-hour job. All the crew are dedicated to their work, and to me and their Captain. I expect you to be the same. Come, I'll take you to meet him. Captain Moorbank is a very fair man, but like me he'll stand no nonsense.'

Tammy followed mutinously as he led the way to the bridge, wondering why she had ever thought Hugo Kane a kind man to take her in. A skivvy was what he was after, someone at his beck and call all hours of the day. The trouble was, at the moment, she had no choice. She had to take the job, whether she wanted it or not.

Captain Moorbank was tall, almost as tall as Hugo Kane, with a certain dominance that made him well suited to his position. His grey hair was cropped short and his blue eyes narrowed as only those of a sailor can be after perpetually squinting into the sun.

His handshake was firm and he greeted her pleasantly enough, but Tammy knew he would be a hard taskmaster and would indeed, as Hugo had said, put up with no funny business among his crew.

On the sun deck Tammy was able to look out across the great expanse of shiny blue ocean and the host of other yachts fringing the edges of the square harbour. Yachts larger than she had ever seen before, each one in itself costing a small fortune.

Hugo Kane must be very rich to own such a superb vessel, she thought, and surprised herself by feeling sudden contempt. Especially if he could afford to spend time here himself when the boat could be earning him money.

She had never had much time for people who did not work, who sat back and let the money roll in. The owner of the company for which she worked was like that, expecting complete dedication from his employees, while he enjoyed himself with the profit of their labour.

'Do you spend much time on your boat, Mr Kane?' she asked.

'I see no reason to own such a vessel and not use it,' he said shortly.

'It must cost an awful lot to keep it here,' she persisted. 'I'm surprised you can afford to lose out on the charter season.'

'If you're questioning my wealth, Miss Swift, I suggest you mind your own business. I've invited some very good friends to spend a few weeks here with me and I'm damn sure I'm not going to allow some chit of a girl tell me what to do.'

'I didn't mean to do that,' she said, half apologetically. 'It was just that—well, I suppose I'm curious. I only know one other man who doesn't need to work.'

His thick brows arched. 'You sound as though you despise him for it.'

'I don't exactly admire him, nor any of the idle rich.'

'And you're placing me in that category?'

Tammy began to wish she had never started the conversation. It really was no business of hers what Hugo Kane did with his time. 'I didn't say that.'

'But you thought it, which is just as bad. I'll thank you, Miss Swift, to keep your opinions to yourself in future. Now, come along, I'll show you what I require you to do.'

A quarter of an hour later Tammy realised why it was that she would never have any time of her own, except when she went to bed. She was expected to keep the entire inside of the ship clean and tidy, which involved, he told her, as well as the rooms she had already seen, the master stateroom and three others which were in use at the moment, also the crew's cabins, although they sometimes did their own. She would also wait at the table and do any other jobs that were asked of her.

'You expect me to do all this by myself?' she queried incredulously when he had finished and they were standing once again on the sun deck.

'Why not? Miss Harriet coped admirably and she was much older than you.'

Miss Harriet sounded a gem. Tammy was not sure that she would be able to live up to her predecessor. 'I expect she was used to this sort of work —I'm not.'

'Are you trying to tell me that it's too much for you?'

His derogatory tone incensed her into a heated

denial. 'Of course not! It's more than I expected, that's all. I didn't realise your boat was so big. Give me a little time to get myself into a routine and I'll manage.'

'My guests won't like it if they find their beds not made or wet towels in their bathrooms.'

Having always been used to looking after herself Tammy could not understand anyone who couldn't do these things for themselves, and she heaved an exasperated sigh. 'I'll do my best, I can't say more.'

He looked at her hard and long and she felt a quiver run through her limbs as those dark eyes penetrated her own. 'You sound subdued,' he observed. 'What's happened to the fiery redhead I first met?'

'My hair is not red,' she cried indignantly. 'It's auburn, and just because it's this colour it doesn't mean to say I have a temper.'

'No?' and his eyes mocked her. 'But I like spirit. It would be a pity to repress it. You're very pretty, especially when you're angry. In fact I would go so far as to say that you're the prettiest "charwoman" I've ever had.'

Tammy's green eyes flashed and she was stung into retorting, 'I thought we'd agreed I wasn't one of those. I don't like the word—it reminds me of flowered overalls and turbans.'

He tilted his head to one side, smiling crookedly. 'You could look rather appealing dressed like that, though I think I preferred the white sheet. You looked like a virgin and your wide green eyes were full of apprehension. Did you think I was going to rape you?'

He was blunt, if nothing else, and Tammy felt the

colour rise in her cheeks. Her thoughts had not stretched that far, but she had to admit that a strange weakness had invaded her limbs and she felt curious as to what it would be like to be kissed by this man, this tall dark, devastating stranger.

'I didn't think anything,' she said a shade defiantly, 'except that you had a nerve coming in without knocking.'

'Oh, come now,' he said. 'No one who's caught in such a compromising situation could be expected not to feel some sort of emotion, whether it was desire, or fear, or whatever.'

'And you think I would tell you what I felt?' she protested, trying hard to hide the embarrassment this conversation caused. 'Really, Mr Kane, a girl has a right to some private thoughts!'

'I'll tell you what I felt, then,' he said calmly, leaning back against the rail and surveying her steadily. 'I wanted to kiss you. I wanted to take you into my arms and feel your body next to mine. Does that surprise you?'

Tammy shrugged with what she hoped was indifference. 'You're human. I suppose any man would feel the same, under the circumstances, but I'm grateful you controlled your emotions.'

'Grateful?' His eyes widened mockingly. 'What would you have done if I hadn't?'

'Screamed,' she said promptly.

'With my lips on yours? Impossible.'

'Then I'd have kicked and scratched like any girl if she was being molested.'

'Interesting!'

The light in his eyes should have warned her what was coming next, but it didn't, and when he pulled her roughly into his arms, pinning her hands at her sides, it was too late to try and withdraw.

His mouth claimed hers in a brutally savage kiss and the only sound that escaped her was a muffled cry. She could feel his hard, lean body pressed against hers, hear the drumming of his heartbeats and her own echoing in unison.

When at length he lifted his head his eyes glittered down into hers and a slow smile flickered the corners of his mouth. 'Where were your objections? You don't look as if you found that unpleasant.'

To be truthful she hadn't. He had aroused in her emotions she had never before known existed, but because of this she hated him and her hand flew up to strike his face. He side-stepped neatly, his smile widening, as though he had expected such a response and had actually enjoyed inciting her.

'That was a rotten thing to do,' she flamed. 'Have you forgotten that you're engaged, that I am too, for that matter?'

'Hugo!' A hurt, petulant voice made them both turn.

Tammy saw a beautiful young woman with dark eyes flashing fire and wide red lips which at this moment were drawn into an unpleasant line. She had long black hair which fell against her face like shining silk. Her cream dress must have cost the earth and her high-heeled black sandals were the perfect complement.

'Andrea.' Hugo did not look in the least disturbed to have been caught with another woman in his arms. 'Come and meet Tammy. I've been showing her the boat. She's quite impressed.'

'But not so impressed with its owner, judging by

her reaction to your kiss. Not all women find you irresistible, darling.' She tucked her arm into his, her face suddenly relaxing, although her eyes were hard as they looked Tammy carefully over.

Hugo gave a careless shrug and covered Andrea's hand with his own. 'Jealous, my pet? No need. As you say, Tammy objects to my attentions being forced upon her. Can you blame me for trying, though, she's a pretty little thing.'

Andrea didn't think so, judging by the way her lips curled. 'You'll never change, will you, darling?' She studied the ring on her finger, the biggest diamond Tammy had ever seen, sparkling now in the early morning sunlight. 'But I don't mind—at least not until we're married, then if you dare go astray——' Her threat tailed off with a tight little laugh and Tammy knew that she was not really amused, was, in fact, as jealous as hell over the attentions he had been paying her, Tammy, but was too cunning to reveal it.

'So,' Andrea continued her appraisal of Tammy, 'this is the poor girl you rescued from Emil's clutches. She looks to me as though she would have no difficulty in looking after herself. Are you sure she needed rescuing, darling? I know you've always been partial to redheads.'

Tammy bit back the impulse to deny her hair was that colour, arguing with Andrea would make matters worse. For the short time she was here perhaps she could pretend to like her, even though she could see that she was a spoilt little rich girl, used to getting her own way.

But what galled most was the way Hugo pampered her. The way he had said, 'Jealous, my pet?'

was sickening, and not at all in keeping with the man he had shown her. They said love did funny things to people, but she would never have believed that Hugo Kane would be soft where a woman was concerned.

'She was clearly new to the game,' said Hugo levelly, 'and being a compatriot of ours I could hardly let her go on with it. You know what Conin's like, he never lets on what he really wants them for until it's too late.'

'Even so, darling, did you have to bring her back here?'

'You forget, my sweet, that Conin has all her possessions. Until I get them back I intend keeping her here where I can keep an eye on her.'

'A sort of father figure,' laughed Andrea, her clear bell-like voice tinkling into the morning air. 'I've never seen you in that light before, but so long as that's all you're going to be to her, I don't mind. How about you, Tammy, does Hugo strike you as a father?'

Compared to the kind gentle soul who had filled her early years and who was now little more than a blurred memory, there was no similarity between them. Tragically Tammy had been orphaned at the age of ten and brought up by an aunt and uncle who had not really wanted her but had considered it their duty. Consequentially when she had become of age they had raised no objections when she said she was going to London.

She looked at Hugo now, at the arrogant tilt to his head, hard dark eyes staring at her aloofly, as though he had never held her in his arms.

The kiss had affected him also, she knew that, yet

to all outward appearances she was nothing, a no-body, something he had picked up and was doing the decent thing by.

'No,' she said bluntly. 'I think he would make a terrible father. He's too masterful by far, thinking he knows what's best for other people when they would thank him for leaving them alone. I'm not so sure I wouldn't have been better off with Emil Conin.'

Andrea arched her fine brows delicately. 'Your protégée is quite a spitfire, darling, when she gets going. Perhaps you ought to have left her with Emil.'

'I can handle her,' he said confidently, and his tone was such that Tammy's chin shot up and her green eyes flashed with unconcealed hatred.

'I'll thank you not to talk about me as though I'm a parcel of baggage! If you'll excuse me, I'll get on with my duties. Oh, and Andrea, thanks for the loan of the clothes—I love the colour. It's not often people with auburn hair can wear red, but I'm just mad about it.'

She walked away, her head held high, aware that they were both watching, and hoped that her parting shot had scored.

CHAPTER THREE

TAMMY had been informed that her services would not be required at breakfast, so when she saw all the guests assembled she decided to go and see to the staterooms. She would have her own breakfast later, if she was hungry. At the moment food was the farthest thought from her mind.

Hugo's kiss had disturbed her more than she cared to admit. It had been so unexpected, yet totally devastating. David's kisses had never done this to her, yet she loved David, so what reason was there for such a reaction?

She collected her cleaning materials from a cupboard near the kitchen and made her way to the master stateroom, Hugo's private domain.

The room was impressive but held no reflection of its occupant. Here was quiet grace, tasteful luxury. Anyone entering and not knowing to whom it belonged would never guess that a man as hatefully dominant as Hugo Kane slept here.

It was large and sumptuous and the whole of the wall behind the big double bed was padded in velvet. Matching it was a gold silk bedspread with long rippling fringes, and the floor was inches deep in wine-coloured carpet. Wall lamps also had burgundy shades, and the gold and white furniture was elegance itself.

Tammy sank down on to one of the chairs to try and gather her muddled thoughts. Hugo had clearly been playing about with her feelings, up there on the deck, perhaps needing to satisfy himself as to what sort of girl she was. Her cheeks flamed when she realised she had not exactly fought off his advances. It was only afterwards when reaction had set in that she felt the urge to pay him back for what he had done. But he wouldn't try it again, of that she was sure. If he thought anything of Andrea, and he must if they were engaged, he would not risk getting into her bad books.

She made the bed, feeling a strange sense of awareness as she plumped the pillow on which Hugo's head had lain, smoothed the sheets which had covered his lean, virile body. There were no pyjamas in sight, so she assumed he slept in the nude, and the clothes he had worn last night had all been put away. This was one thing in his favour, she supposed, his tidiness. It would make her own job easier, if nothing else.

Twin bathrooms led off the stateroom, each expensively tiled in marble and onyx. The fittings were gold and she was almost frightened to touch, but nevertheless she could not help feeling a certain sense of satisfaction when everything was once more gleaming and orderly.

She had spent so long in Hugo's room that the other guests had already finished their breakfasts and were gathering up magazines and towels and anything else they might need for a morning on the deck of this luxury motor yacht.

How lucky they were, thought Tammy, as she apologised for not having done their rooms, to have a friend like Hugo to invite them for such a wonderful holiday. On the other hand, perhaps to them it wasn't so wonderful. They appeared to be monied people in their own right and no doubt they took this sort of thing for granted, whereas she found it all tremendously exciting and out of this world.

She wondered what David's reaction would be if he saw her now. Would he be annoyed that she had got involved with people she did not know? It occurred to her that he would be writing to her at the Pascals'. Would Simone and Pierre open her letter and tell him she was not there, or would it be forwarded to her London flat where it would remain until she returned?

She rather hoped it would be the latter. She didn't want David worrying about her and maybe cutting short his business trip, thus jeopardising his chance of success. Maybe she ought to write to him, perhaps concoct some story which would explain her leaving the Pascals in such a hurry.

The Murrays, one of the couples staying on the boat, told her they came from Scotland and ran their own textile business. They were very sympathetic towards Tammy, having heard of her plight from Hugo over breakfast, and Maggie Murray soon made it clear that if she could help in any way she would, as she appreciated how difficult it was being thrust into a new job without any training.

But the other guests, Keith and Penny Anderson, Londoners who had settled in Monaco after having won a small fortune on the pools, Tammy didn't like at all. Their wealth had gone to their heads and they thought themselves a cut above the likes of Tammy. Penny Anderson was the untidiest person Tammy had ever come across and it took her twice as long to tidy her room as it had the Murrays'.

Andrea too was untidy, but Tammy had not expected anything else here, being half inclined to believe that the other girl had done it on purpose.

When all the staterooms were finished, each one in the luxury class though none of them equalling Hugo's own, Tammy went down to the lower deck prepared to do the crew's cabins. It was a delightful surprise to find all the beds made and the rooms tidy, and she made a mental note to thank them all for helping her out on this her first day.

Back up on the main deck Tammy felt she had earned a break, and going into the kitchen asked Chips whether she could make herself a slice of toast and a cup of coffee.

'Have you had no breakfast, child?' he asked at once, concerned, and then answered the question himself. 'But of course you haven't, you were with Hugo when we had ours. We usually eat early, before the guests are up, after that there isn't time.'

He pushed her on to a stool and slid two slices of bread beneath the grill, and deftly whisked two eggs until they foamed. In no time at all her toast was topped with steaming golden scrambled egg, and he was quite prepared to cook more if she needed it.

She laughed protestingly. 'This is fine, Chips. I never eat much in the mornings.'

'Most important meal of the day,' he said brusquely. 'You can't work on an empty stomach.'

Looking at his bulging middle Tammy could well believe that he enjoyed good food, and guessed he would go out of his way to try and see that everyone else did the same.

Tammy had just finished her coffee when Hugo

appeared, his face as black as thunder. 'So there you are!' he bellowed. 'The saloons need cleaning. It will soon be time for lunch and there's no work been done.'

'I've finished the staterooms,' Tammy protested, her wide eyes flickering distastefully in his direction. 'Surely you don't begrudge me a bite of breakfast?'

'At this hour of the day?' looking at the heavy gold watch which adorned his wrist.

'Pardon me, sir,' interrupted Chips, 'but she was with you earlier when we had ours. The poor girl must eat, she looked ready to faint away.'

Hugo treated the chef to a cold stare. 'I'll thank you not to interfere, my good man. Miss Swift is here to work. If she misses her meals then it's too bad.'

Chips sighed and said no more, but Tammy was determined not to let this tyrant treat her like a galley slave. 'I resent your attitude, Mr Kane,' she said strongly. 'As Chips said, if I don't eat I won't have the strength to keep up with the work.'

'Ah,' he pounced, 'so you're admitting it's too much for you?'

'No, I'm not, but I know my rights. All employees are allowed a mid-morning break, so if I missed breakfast then this can count as my elevenses, or whatever you like to call it. I've finished now, so if you've said all you have to say I'll get on with my work.' She jumped to her feet and stared belligerently into his face, challenging him to continue his argument.

To her surprise he laughed and gave her a playful pat on the bottom. 'What a fireball you are! Get going before I'm tempted to hit you harder.'

. Tammy went, knowing that his amusement was
only a temporary thing and that if she had dared to
defy him further he would not hesitate to carry out
his threat. She assumed from Chips' look of total
amazement that he had never seen his boss acting in
this high-handed manner before, and she wondered
whether it was something he kept especially for her.
Perhaps no one else ever stuck up to him, perhaps
the rest of the crew were all meek little yes-men,
who did his bidding with no question. He would not
find her so co-operative, not if he insisted on treating her like this. It wasn't as if she was being
punished for something. She was in fact doing him a
favour, even if he had done her one by extracting
her from the villainous Emil Conin.

Her heart full of bitterness towards Hugo,
Tammy vented her anger on the smooth wood of the
dining table.

'You'll rub it away if you continue like that,' came
a mocking voice over her shoulder. 'Do you always
polish with such gusto?'

Tammy smiled wryly as Eddie came into her line
of vision. 'I need to get rid of my temper. That man
is absolutely impossible! Do you know he tore a
strip off me because I dared take ten minutes'
break?

Eddie looked puzzled and ran his fingers through
short brown hair. 'That doesn't sound like Hugo.
He's a bit short-tempered at times, but he's a very
fair man, doesn't usually mind any of us taking five
minutes so long as our work isn't suffering.'

'Then he must have taken a dislike to me.'
Tammy paused in her polishing and stared at Eddie,

her pretty green eyes confused. 'He couldn't say I hadn't done my quota, though I suppose he was concerned that the saloons wouldn't be ready before lunch.'

The chief steward draped his arm lightly about Tammy's waist. 'Never mind, my darling, you can always come to me for consolation if things get difficult. How about going ashore with me tonight for a quiet drink somewhere?'

'How can we?' asked Tammy crossly. 'Hugo says we're allowed no time off. We're on duty twenty-four hours a day.'

'He said that?' Eddie stared, astonished, his hand falling from her waist and again ruffling his springy brown hair. 'He certainly does have it in for you! We have two evenings off a week and one weekend a month. I wonder why he said that?'

Tammy wondered too. It was not a comforting thought that he was treating her differently from everyone else. What motive had he for doing it, what was he hoping to achieve?

'If I was you I'd tackle him about it,' continued Eddie, 'unless you'd like me to do it for you? It's not fair! He shouldn't treat you in this manner. In fact I think it's downright disgusting, and I've half a mind to tell him so myself.'

'Yes, Marchant?' boomed Hugo's voice directly behind them, and they both turned as though drawn by a puppeteer's strings. 'You've a mind to tell me what? Has Miss Swift been crying on your shoulder, telling you what an ogre I am, without a kind thought in my head? You don't understand the position, and I'd thank you to keep your nose out of Miss Swift's affairs.

'As for you, Tammy,' turning to look at her coldly, 'next time you have a grudge against me I suggest you approach me yourself. I'm a reasonable man, even though it would appear you don't think so.'

Tammy didn't know what to say. She was too embarrassed that she had been caught talking about him to try and defend herself.

She stared for a few seconds, but as his cold hard eyes penetrated her, her embarrassment disappeared, to be replaced by anger. Who did he think he was, speaking to her like this? She had not asked him for the job, he had more or less forced her into it, so why shouldn't she defend herself?

'I wasn't complaining to Eddie,' she said fiercely, 'it just came up in conversation. But as we're talking about the subject, I may as well say that I don't think it very noble of you to make me work all day and every day when the rest of the crew have time off.'

Hugo frowned savagely. 'If you wish to discuss your terms of employment then I should prefer to do it alone.' He looked at the chief steward. 'Marchant, will you kindly leave?'

Eddie, who had been so brave behind Hugo's back, walked quietly out of the saloon, and Tammy felt disappointed that he had not stayed to champion her, had not even so much as attempted to put in a word on her behalf.

As soon as they were alone she attacked Hugo spiritedly. 'If you're going to try and make excuses, it won't work. Eddie's told me about the crew's hours, and I demand that I have the same.'

Hugo leaned back against the edge of the table, his tall frame dominating the room. 'You're not a regular crew member, therefore I'm at liberty to quote whatever terms I like.'

Tammy grudgingly supposed this was true, but even so she had no intention of allowing him to dictate to her. 'And do you call that fair, keeping me penned up here when everyone else is enjoying themselves ashore?'

Hugo studied her face, her green eyes flashing fire and her auburn hair swinging across her cheeks as she tossed her head angrily.

There was a harsh bitterness about his lips and she wondered how she could ever have felt grateful to him for rescuing her. It was like falling out of the proverbial frying pan into the fire and at the moment she was not sure which was the lesser of the two evils.

'I have my reasons,' he said coolly.

The fact that he was able to control his temper, even though she knew he was inwardly seething, made Tammy all the more heedless of what she said. 'And I expect those are purely selfish. If they weren't you wouldn't work me like a slave. Cheap labour, is that what you're after?'

'Not so cheap as what Conin was prepared to pay,' he said grimly. 'He makes a fortune out of girls like you, and I don't suppose he was very pleased when he discovered I'd taken you away from him.'

'He looked pleased when he saw us leaving the casino together.'

'That was because he thought I was going to help swell his bank balance. I'd have liked to see his face when you didn't go back.'

The very fact that Emil Conin had approved of her accompanying Hugo made Tammy think that this dark handsome devil in front of her must have done this sort of thing before. How else would Emil Conin know him, and why would he have given them his blessing if he hadn't thought that Hugo Kane wasn't buying his pleasure? The thought made her shudder and involuntarily she stepped back, a look of loathing crossing her expressive face.

Hugo smiled grimly. 'For that reason I think it's best you don't go ashore, not until you're ready to return to England. If Conin gets his hands on you again I hate to think what might happen. He's not a pleasant man once he's been crossed.'

'I'm not frightened of Emil Conin,' declared Tammy courageously. 'Besides, I wouldn't go alone. As a matter of fact Eddie Marchant has already asked me to go for a drink tomorrow night.'

'And some use he'd be if it came to a showdown between him and Conin. He's a good lad, but not tough enough for the likes of hardened racketeers.'

'You're exaggerating,' scoffed Tammy.

'I'm merely warning you, but you're such a stubborn little thing you refuse to accept that I know what's best.' He moved away from the table towards her, and Tammy, thinking he was going to touch her, stepped back yet again.

He frowned darkly, his eyes cold and glittering. 'I know exactly what's running through your mind, and if it pleases you to think that I'm that sort of person, then go ahead. All I can say is that you're not a very good judge of character.'

Tammy shrugged. 'Maybe not, but my instinct tells me now not to trust you.'

'Did it tell you to trust Emil Conin?'

She stared at him defiantly. 'What would you say

if I said yes? Would you send me back and tell me to get on with it, or would you still offer me your protection?'

'I would say you were a fool,' he said savagely, 'a damn silly fool who should never have been allowed out of England by herself.'

Before she had time to move he had grasped her by the shoulders, his thumbs digging painfully into the soft flesh below her bone. 'If I were your fiancé I'd put you over my knee and give you the good hiding you deserve, perhaps knock some sense into that thick head of yours.'

'But you're not,' she blazed back, 'so please let me go. You can't treat me like this, I won't let you!'

For an answer he shook her, so violently that her teeth rattled. 'I will treat you exactly how I want to while you're on board the *Flying Queen*, and if it means I have to personally supervise you to see that you don't go ashore, then I shall do just that. The only time you will go is when I'm with you.'

'And what's Andrea going to say to that?' she asked sharply. 'I don't think she'll like it. I'm on her hate list already. If you pay me more attention than you do her there's going to be all hell let loose.'

'I can handle Andrea,' he said tightly, letting her go with an abruptness that sent her stumbling backwards across the room. The back of her knees caught a chair and she sat down heavily, glaring up with intense hatred at the dark giant who was glaring down as though he too loathed the sight of her.

'I don't know why you're bothering,' she cried raggedly, wondering why she felt near to tears. 'Why don't you let me go, forget you ever saw me? I'm sure your life would be a whole lot smoother.'

His thick brows arched. 'I've no doubt it would, but unfortunately for me I have a conscience, so, Miss Tamsin Swift, we're stuck together whether you like it or not. I suggest you get on with your work and as soon as lunch is over we'll go into Monte Carlo and get you those clothes you so desperately need.' His lips quirked as he added, 'And they certainly won't be red. That outfit clashes so discordantly with your red hair that it's no wonder you're in a temper.'

'My hair is not red!' flashed Tammy, but she might have been talking to herself, since Hugo had disappeared. Trust him to have the last word, she fumed, as she struggled to her feet and continued to polish the table.

Shortly before lunchtime Tammy made her way into the kitchen. Chips was busily engaged in the final preparations for the meal, but looked up when she entered and smiled, his round face holding more than a hint of compassion.

'Hope you didn't take that little scene this morning too much to heart,' he said. 'I've never known Hugo like that before. It makes me wonder why he brought you aboard if he's going to be nasty to you.'

'Me too,' agreed Tammy with a wry smile, 'but I'm not going to let him browbeat me, and he knows it. Perhaps he's not used to being answered back, I don't know, but he certainly won't find me a weak timid little thing who'll do his bidding without question.'

Chips laughed. 'Atta girl, that's the spirit! Now you'd best get on and lay the table, or you'll have the guests after you as well as the boss.'

'That's what I wanted to ask, how many will there be? Is anyone out?'

'No,' he answered. 'The Murrays and the Andersons are both here today, though sometimes they do go ashore and dine in the town. They're supposed to tell me if they're going to be absent, but they don't always, especially that Anderson woman. So it pays to keep your eyes and ears skinned, that way you don't go to all the trouble of cooking food that's not wanted.'

Tammy could well imagine Penny Anderson not bothering to inform Chips of her whereabouts, and as she set the table she pondered over Hugo counting such a despicable woman among his friends.

The Murrays were completely opposite—just as wealthy, but having earned their money the hard way. Hugo had told her a little about them, about the textile business his grandfather had founded and which was now thriving with several mills scattered about Scotland. Both of the Murrays worked in the family firm and this holiday was their first for many years.

She stood back and surveyed the table, pleased with the effect of the plates with their bright marigold design against the deeper orange of the place mats. The crystal glasses and silver cutlery gleamed and a low flower arrangement of white and orange flowers completed the scene.

The table was finished when Andrea sauntered into the dining room. She contrived to look surprised on seeing the other girl, but Tammy had a feeling that this meeting had been engineered and that there was something Hugo's fiancée wanted to say. She did not have to wait long to find out.

'Ah, Tammy, I'm glad I've caught you alone. I want to talk to you.'

Andrea looked pleasant enough, but there was an

artificialness to her smile that put Tammy immediately on her guard. 'Can't it wait?' she asked abruptly. 'I'm busy at the moment.'

The dark-haired girl looked down at the table. 'It looks ready to me.'

'I have other duties,' retorted Tammy acidly. 'If you'll excuse me, some other time perhaps.'

But Andrea was not going to let her go so easily. She stood in the doorway, effectively blocking the exit. 'I think now is as good a time as any, before you begin to get the wrong idea about Hugo.'

'Hugo?' Tammy assumed a look of surprise, although she wasn't, not in the least. It had been obvious from the beginning that Andrea would regard as suspicious any girl Hugo brought back on the boat. It didn't have to be Tammy, it could be anyone. It was just her bad luck that it happened to be her.

She folded her arms and faced the other girl. 'What gives you the idea that I might be even remotely interested in your fiancé? Didn't my reaction to his advances this morning convince you that he's not my type? As a matter of fact I'm engaged too. Didn't Hugo tell you that?'

She held out her hand so that the girl could see for herself her diamond and sapphire ring. It was nothing compared with the diamond Andrea wore, but even so it was sufficient to make the other girl look first of all surprised and then a whole lot more friendly.

'Hugo never told me,' she mused. 'I can't think why, unless he was trying to make me jealous. Isn't that just like him, the adorable brute? Forgive me, Tammy, for being suspicious,' and she disappeared as swiftly as she had arrived.

Adorable brute! Tammy's lips curled at this description as she made her way back to the kitchen. She could think of many adjectives to describe Hugo, but adorable certainly didn't rate among them.

The meal was more successful than Tammy had expected, perhaps because the guests took into account the fact that she was new at the job; even when she almost tipped a dish of consommé on to Penny Anderson's lap the woman merely smiled.

No doubt the liberal quantity of wine she had consumed had mellowed her, but Hugo himself had not been so kind. His smouldering dark eyes had cut through her, and without a word spoken Tammy knew that should she make another slip she would not be let off leniently.

What does he expect, she asked herself angrily, when I've never done this sort of thing before? If he can do any better let him come and do it himself!

She took extra care, though, after that, but it was difficult with Hugo's eyes watching her every move. Andrea too noticed the way he looked at Tammy, and a frown marred the smooth perfection of her forehead, and she did all in her power to keep him engaged in conversation.

It was a relief when the meal was over and the guests departed, leaving Tammy to clear the table and then join the other crew members for their own lunch.

She had just started to eat when Hugo appeared.

'Are you ready?' he asked brusquely.

She was tempted to say, 'Does it look as though I am?' but instead she pushed her plate away and stood up, ignoring Chips' outraged expression and the astonishment of the others. 'As soon as you like,' she said, and her voice was as sweet as honey.

Hugo looked suspicious but said nothing, and once they were off the boat he ushered her into his waiting car. The big blue Mercedes was as opulent as the *Flying Queen* and Tammy guessed that this man never did anything by halves. Her lips tightened. It did not seem fair that some people should have so much money while others had so little.

Her aunt and uncle had been forced to live on a very tight budget, her uncle often being away from work for weeks at a time with the chronic bronchitis that had plagued him all his life. Consequently Tammy had never owned anything of any great value, or even travelled far from her home town of Derby until she had gone to London.

It was not until she met David that she had begun to see something of her native England, and her honeymoon in France was something about which she had dreamed for a long time. David was not short of money, though judging by Hugo's standards he was still relatively poor, but she had enjoyed the freedom that little bit of extra cash had given her.

But to have as much as Hugo had, enough to buy a complete stranger a whole new wardrobe of clothes without counting the cost, and to live for weeks at a time on a luxury yacht without ever thinking of work, this was beyond her comprehension, and she could not help despising him for it.

'Is something wrong?' he asked, his deep velvet voice suddenly breaking into her thoughts. 'You're looking very angry. I thought any girl would be excited at the thought of shopping for clothes.'

Tammy glared at him. 'I'm not any girl, as you've

probably realised. You might as well know, I don't like the idea of you buying me anything.'

'But under the circumstances you're having to force yourself to accept, is that it?' he asked cuttingly.

'I've no alternative,' she snapped. 'How soon will it be before you get my things back off Emil Conin?'

Hugo shrugged laconically. 'I can't rush things. At the moment he's probably smarting so much that I whisked you from under his nose that if I dared turn up there'd be a first-class brawl.'

Tammy sniffed. 'Are you scared of him?'

'Not in the least,' he returned calmly. 'But I don't like fighting in public.'

'Can't you find out where he lives, couldn't you go there?' asked Tammy persistently, annoyed by Hugo's indifference. It was all right for him, it wasn't his belongings that had gone missing. It was embarrassing to have to be beholden to this man without so much as two pence to her name.

'In good time,' came his smooth reply. 'What's the rush? You're being well looked after. If there's anything I forget, or anything you want in particular, just cry out and it will be yours.'

It was easy for him to talk, he wasn't on the begging end. She felt like hitting him, and only by clasping her hands together in her lap could she stop herself.

He halted the car suddenly and Tammy realised they were there. It hadn't really been worth the ride, they could have walked. She asked him why they hadn't.

'Because,' he said patiently, as one might explain to a child, 'we have to carry the parcels back. Unless you have hidden strength in those slender arms I think you'll agree this is by the far the best way.'

He made her question sound stupid and Tammy's head was held high as she walked at his side. She felt dwarfed beside this giant of a man and had to take little trotting steps to keep up with him.

The town was small with no more than a few streets comprising its entirety. Hugo told her that Monaco itself was only about half the size of Central Park in New York, but as she had no idea how big that was it meant nothing to her. She merely smiled, acknowledging his statement, and hoped that she looked as though she knew what he was talking about.

He halted outside a shop where none of the dresses in the window were priced. Tammy herself had always avoided this sort of place as she knew they were always more expensive than shops who did show prices.

'Here we are,' he said. 'Madame Dubois is a friend of mine. Tell her I sent you and she'll put you right. I'll meet you back here in two hours. Will that be long enough?'

Tammy nodded. 'More than enough.' It wouldn't take her that long to choose a few clothes to last until her own were recovered. It would in fact be a pity to buy too many when she had a suitcase full of new things that were originally intended for her honeymoon, and which she had brought with her in a gesture of angry defiance when David had so callously postponed their wedding.

But once inside the shop she got carried away at the sight of so many colourful, beautiful dresses, skirts and blouses, and before she knew what was happening had ordered so many different things that she suddenly took fright and would look at no more, in spite of Madame Dubois' insistence that Monsieur Kane would not mind.

Although the shop had a small frontage, inside it was like a miniature department store and when she had finished in the dress department Tammy found herself being shown shoes, and then underwear, and lastly cosmetics.

She felt like Cinderella at the ball with all these new and wonderful things happening to her, and wondered whether it was all a dream from which she would suddenly awake and find herself back in her London flat.

When Hugo appeared inside the shop it astonished her to find that her two hours were up. It had been the shortest and most exhilarating two hours of her life, and her pleasure was reflected in her face as she watched him approaching across the expensively carpeted floor.

'Ah, Monsieur Kane,' exclaimed Madame Dubois at once. 'We have fixed your little friend up perfectly. No problem. She has a beautiful figure which shows off our clothes to their best advantage.' She accentuated her words with typical French movements of her hands, making Tammy feel as though she was an extra special customer.

Perhaps she was! Perhaps all Hugo's *friends* were special customers. She could not help wondering whether this was not the first time he had done this sort of thing. Madame Dubois had not seemed surprised when she explained her situation, even though Tammy had thought she would.

Her distrust of Hugo Kane deepened and some

of the happiness died from her face. He eyed her consideringly for a few moments before turning to the older woman. 'Thank you so much. I'm once again indebted to you, Madame Dubois. Please have everything packed and put into my car.'

There was no mention of money, noted Tammy. Not even, 'Send the account to me.' It was something taken for granted. Perhaps it was done in all the best circles, who was she to know?

'I expect you could do with a drink?' Hugo took her arm and led her from the shop. 'There's a charming hotel over the road. We'll go there while we're waiting for your purchases.'

Tammy mutely allowed herself to be ushered out to the ultra-smart hotel, following the attentive waiter to a table on the terrace where she could look down the palm-lined street. It was thronged with holidaymakers, happy, laughing people, with apparently not a care in the world. That was how she should have been, she thought bitterly.

Hugo rattled something off in French and the waiter went away. He settled back into his seat, regarding her steadily. 'Now tell me what's on your mind. You looked like a cat who'd stolen the cream when I came into the shop, but your face changed dramatically when you saw me. Why?'

'It isn't because I'm not grateful,' said Tammy at once, feeling all of a sudden that she was being needlessly rude. 'I love all the new clothes, but——' She faltered, unsure how to go on.

'But you object to me buying them,' he finished for her, his voice deepening with quick anger. 'What are you, a prude? You can't afford to turn down my offer, you know that, so why not accept it in the manner in which it was intended?'

He made her sound objectionable, but rather than accede that he was right Tammy replied hotly, 'How would you like it if you had to rely on someone else to keep you? It's embarrassing, to say the least. It wouldn't have been so bad if you'd brought me say a couple of dresses and a pair of shoes—but no, you have to go the whole hog. Are you trying to prove how much money you have, or something? Or is it my friendship you're trying to buy, for some obscure reason known only to yourself?'

Realising that she had raised her voice and other people were looking their way with interest, Tammy subsided, finishing with a loud whisper, 'It won't work. If you want to know, I hate your guts, and the sooner I'm back in England the better!'

He looked unperturbed, regarding her calmly as though she had said nothing that could in any way hurt him. Only the pulsing in his jaw told her that he was not unaffected. 'You're a strange creature, Tamsin Swift. No other girl has ever reacted to me in this way. You intrigue me, you make me want to find out what makes you tick.'

'Perhaps they were impressed by your money,' she said scathingly, 'that's the difference. It must be quite a novelty to find someone who actually despises you because of your wealth.'

'It's different,' he admitted. 'A challenge, perhaps?'

'What, to try and make me like you?' Her wide green eyes were indignant, blazing with angry colour. 'What about your fiancée?'

'What about Andrea?' The cool grey eyes met her own, smouldering beneath dark brows, and although she hated to admit it, there was something about them that caused a quickening of her pulses.

'Sh 's already tried to warn me off you,' she snapped, though what gave her the idea I might be interested I don't know. It had escaped her notice that I too wear an engagement ring—perhaps I ought to remind you that I do have a boy-friend and he wouldn't take kindly to another man showing interest in me.'

'Perfectly normal,' shrugged Hugo, 'but our circumstances are slightly different, don't you think? On board the *Flying Queen* we're bound to come into close contact. You won't be able to avoid me, in the same way that I shall not be able to keep away from you. Besides, if your young man has the appalling bad manners to let you roam France on your own, then he deserves the consequences. Surely he didn't expect a pretty girl like you to remain on her own for long?'

'He trusted me,' she said indignantly, 'rightly so. I have no intention of becoming involved with you, or anyone else.'

'You almost got yourself involved with Conin,' he mocked. 'What would the dear fiancé have said about that, I wonder? I expect he'd have been scandalised and want nothing more to do with you.'

This was unfortunately too near the mark for Tammy's liking. David would have been shocked, and he would almost certainly have blamed her, and they would have ended up having yet another row. But she wouldn't admit this to Hugo, not for anything would she let him know that David was anything less than perfect in her eyes. 'He wouldn't!' she returned heatedly. 'David would understand.'

'He'd have to be a saint to do so,' he said explosively. 'I'm damn sure I wouldn't if a girl of mine got herself tied up in such a racket. She'd either have to be a gullible fool, in which case I would want nothing more to do with her anyway, or enter into the whole thing with her eyes open and say hang the consequences, I'm out for a good time.'

His mouth twisted bitterly as he spoke, and Tammy wondered into which category he placed her. 'How do you see me?' she asked caustically, heedless of the fact that their waiter had returned with a pot of tea and a plateful of delicious-looking cakes.

'I don't think that matters,' he said. 'Would you like to be mother?'

It piqued her that he should treat her question with such indifference, and her resentment increased as she poured the tea into delicate china cups. She sipped hers, maintaining a mutinous silence, but the hot, strong liquid didn't taste like English tea, and she pulled a face, setting down her cup and selecting a particularly gooey-looking cream cake from the middle of the plate.

'I'm glad you don't have to watch your figure,' he said lightly. 'Andrea has to be careful what she eats —or at least that's what she tells me.'

'How soon are you getting married?' asked Tammy bluntly, licking cream from round her lips and taking another bite.

Hugo shrugged, pulling his mouth down at the corners. 'We haven't discussed it.'

'I bet Andrea would like it to be soon,' she insisted, trying to see how deep his involvement with this girl went. He appeared to treat her very off-handedly, at least when he wasn't with her. When they were together there was a sickening sweetness about him that was somehow out of character, making her wonder how sincere he was, and whether he would eventually marry Andrea or whether he was simply playing with her feelings with the intention of dropping her later.

He laughed harshly. 'Tomorrow wouldn't be too soon for Andrea.'

'Then why don't you?'

'I don't love her,' he said calmly. 'It's as simple as that.'

His admittance surprised Tammy and she paused in the act of chewing. 'Then why did you get engaged?'

'Shall we say I was tricked into it?' he replied, and for a brief moment he looked cross, but the expression soon faded and he smiled. 'So you see, it suits me to pretend—for the moment. When the time is right I shall very gently break off our arrangement, unless Andrea does it first.'

'I can't see her doing that,' said Tammy. 'She's besotted with you.'

'Until she meets someone else,' came the smooth reply. 'Andrea's in love with money, nothing else. Anyone with the right bank balance and a reasonably presentable appearance will do. If you stay long enough you'll see for yourself.'

'That's a laugh! A few more days and with any luck I shall be off.'

'It will take longer than that to persuade Conin to relinquish your luggage. Time enough, perhaps, for us to get to know one another better?'

Tammy finished her cake and wiped her mouth

on a napkin. 'I hate to dash your hopes, Mr Kane, but there's no chance of that. Even if you don't love Andrea I *do* love David, and I have no intention of two-timing him.'

Even as she spoke Tammy knew that her feelings for David had undergone a dramatic change during the last twelve hours. And there was only one man who could be responsible for it! Devilishly handsome, with a piratical air, and a strong physical attraction that could not be ignored.

Ninety-nine per cent of the time she hated him, but there was that one per cent that could not help a begrudging admiration. He was easily the most manly man she had ever met, throwing David right into the shade, and though she did not like the thought that her head might be turned by him, she could foresee an almighty struggle with herself to keep him out of her mind, especially now she knew that he did not love Andrea and was a completely free agent.

CHAPTER FOUR

BACK on the *Flying Queen* Tammy wasted no time in changing into one of her new dresses. A pale green cotton with a tied halter neck and a billowing skirt, she knew it made her look far more attractive than the red shirt and slacks. It was cooler too, she argued with herself, knowing almost instinctively that Andrea would think she had dressed up purposely.

The afternoon had gone so quickly that it was virtually time for dinner, and Tammy just managed to run the Hoover along the corridors and make sure the two main saloons were tidy before setting the table.

This time she chose a plain white china dinner service, using brilliant red place mats and a centre-piece of anemones. She had no idea where the flowers came from, but there was a plentiful supply in a corner of the kitchen. Exotic blooms, flowers out of season, just about any flower you could think of. She shuddered to think of the amount of money spent on this item alone.

Eddie joined her and Chips in the kitchen as they were waiting for the guests to put in an appearance. Everything was ready, and if there was anything Chips hated it was having to keep the meal warm. 'It's not the first time they've done this,' he grumbled. 'It's always the same, especially when that Anderson woman is staying here. She doesn't give a damn how long she keeps me waiting, but anything wrong with the food and she's the first to complain.'

Pulling a face behind his back, the chief steward said, 'Never mind, Chips, the more they leave the more there is for us.'

'That's not the point,' said Chips huffily. 'No good cook likes his food spoilt.'

'You worry too much,' said Eddie lightly. 'How about the *Amaryllis*—that's the yacht next to us,' he added for Tammy's benefit, 'their cook was telling me that sometimes the guests don't turn up at all, and that's after he's cooked a full-scale meal. At least you never have that problem, Chippy, my fellow.'

Chips sighed and turned away to check his oven.

Eddie grinned at Tammy. 'Poor man, it's the end of the world if he has to keep anything warm for more than five minutes.'

Tammy said, 'I sympathise with him. I know exactly how he feels.'

'Trust you to champion him,' he grumbled good-naturedly, 'but enough about food, allow me to say how charming you look this evening.'

'Thank you, kind sir,' dimpled Tammy. 'It was a relief to get out of those awful red clothes.'

'But I'm as jealous as hell that you went out with the boss,' he continued, sliding his arm across her bare shoulders. 'Have you managed to persuade him to give you time off?'

Tammy shook her head. 'It's not really worth it, I won't be here that long. Just as soon as my luggage is recovered I shall go home.'

'Then I haven't much time to waste,' he said, cupping his hand beneath her chin and forcing her lips up to meet his.

His kiss evoked no response from Tammy. She liked Eddie, but not in that way, and she struggled to free herself. 'This is neither the time nor the place for such behaviour,' she said crossly.

'Then meet me tonight,' he said plaintively, 'when your work is finished. I must have some time alone with you—you're the only available female on the boat.'

'Thanks for the compliment,' said Tammy drily, inwardly laughing.

'I didn't mean that how it sounded,' he said, immediately apologetic, 'but Tammy, please say you'll see me. If you don't,' he put a hand to his heart dramatically, 'I shall throw myself overboard.'

Tammy laughed. 'You idiot, you haven't known me long enough to know how you feel about me. You like female company, full stop. But yes, I will. A drink on deck about ten sounds fine.'

Soon after that the guests began to filter in and Tammy was kept busy. As she had guessed, Andrea eyed her jealously in her new green dress, and Tammy vainly hoped that Hugo might pass some comment. But for all the notice he took she could have been wearing an old sack. His full attention was divided between his guests and Andrea, and Tammy was just the waitress who kept things running smoothly.

His disregard hurt, particularly after he had said this afternoon that he would like to get to know her better. It was perverse of her, she knew, especially after she had taken such great pains to tell him that she loved David, but no woman likes to think herself ignored, even by the man she professes to hate.

Hugo and his friends remained at the table long after their meal, drinking coffee and sipping liqueurs, talking and laughing. All the time Tammy was at their constant beck and call, growing more and more hungry as the minutes passed.

Her half-eaten lunch had not been compensated for by the cream cake and now she felt ravenous, willing the party at the table to hurry so that she could eat her own dinner.

Finally they departed. Hugo was the last to leave but at the door he turned back, 'Oh, Tammy, the Andersons' room wants doing again. See to it, please, as soon as you've cleared the table.'

He disappeared before she could speak, but

Tammy was furious and her eyes blazed with deep vivid colour as she stacked the cups and saucers on the tray with little regard that they were of wafer-thin bone china.

That woman! she fumed. What had she been doing that her cabin needed cleaning? Wasn't she capable of doing it for herself? Surely it wasn't her job to do it more than once in the same day?

These questions came bubbling to the surface and had Hugo remained for her response she would have hurled them at him regardless of the consequences. She did not count herself as the normal run-of-the-mill dogsbody on this ship; she was different and should be treated as such. All she was doing was helping him out until he could get someone permanent. Didn't he care that by such treatment she might down her tools and refuse to work at all?

Or would she? Her position really was very precarious and Hugo was quite capable of turning her off and leaving her to fend for herself. How far would she get? The trouble was she was too gullible. She had believed Emil Conin when he had said he could help her, and look where that had landed her!

She grimaced bitterly. She was stuck with this job whether she liked it or not, and by flagrantly disregarding his orders she would only be getting herself into deeper trouble.

Suddenly she wished David was here. Perhaps she ought to write fully and let him know what had happened instead of the polite little note she had already scribbled telling him that she was having a wonderful time.

When she slammed the tray down in the kitchen Chips looked at her in surprise. 'Whatever's the matter, Tammy, something gone wrong? Never mind, come and eat your meal, I've got it all ready —you must be starving.'

'There's no chance of that.' She tossed her head savagely so that the neat twist of curls she had pinned on top came loose and her hair cascaded about her shoulders in deep shining waves. 'Mrs Anderson wants her room done, if you please! Did they treat Miss Harriet like this? If so it's no wonder she went down sick—I should think they worked her to death!'

Chips grimaced sympathetically. 'Hurry along then, it shouldn't take you long. I'll keep your dinner warm.'

Penny Anderson's room looked as though a whirlwind had hit it. There were clothes everywhere, strewn about the bed and across chairs, some even on the floor. Expensive new clothes all treated with as little disregard as if she had bought them in a jumble sale.

Tammy's only conclusion was that the woman had been indecisive about what to wear, discounting one thing after another until her wardrobe was more or less empty. It was no wonder she was late for dinner, but a more heartbreaking thought was, how often did she do this?

It took almost half an hour to put everything away neatly and make sure the room was once more tidy. In Tammy's eyes it was sacrilege to treat such a beautiful room in this manner. The furnishings were the height of luxury with rich velvet drapes and deep-piled wall-to-wall carpeting. The wardrobes were mirror-fronted and the dressing table too had a huge mirror with a built-in lamp that flattered the user's face.

By the time she had finished it was after ten and she was not sure now that she could face a huge meal. Besides, Eddie was waiting for her, and after promising to meet him she did not like to keep him waiting.

But Chips insisted that she had something to eat and when she refused the dinner he made her a chicken salad with thinly sliced bread generously spread with butter.

She felt better after that, not nearly so cross, conscious only that Eddie must think she had stood him up. It was a wonder he had not tried to find her.

When she went up on deck she found out why. He was deep in conversation with Hugo. 'Eddie, I'm sorry,' she began immediately. 'Duty called, and of course that comes before pleasure.'

The irony in her voice was lost on Hugo and he glanced sharply at her. 'I seem to remember telling you, Miss Swift, only a little over twelve hours ago, that I want no familiarity between members of the crew. I've just been telling Marchant the same thing, though I doubt he'll remember it. His memory is conveniently short, but I don't expect yours to be the same. Do you understand?'

Tammy tilted her chin arrogantly. 'No, I don't, Mr Kane. My work is done now, and so, I presume, is Eddie's, so I don't see why we shouldn't meet each other socially. We're still on the ship if you need us, you have no argument.'

'Except that I don't like my rules broken,' he said stiffly.

'It strikes me,' persisted Tammy, 'that you make up your rules to suit yourself, like telling me I couldn't have any time off, when I know full well that everyone else does.'

'I thought I'd explained that,' he grated impatiently. 'I think the best thing you can do now, Miss Swift, is go to bed. You've had a busy day, doing work to which you're unaccustomed, and I shall expect you up at seven in the morning.'

Tammy glanced at Eddie, hoping for his support, but as usual in Hugo's presence he was the meek and obedient employee. Her lips tightened as she tossed her head scornfully. 'I'll go when I'm good and ready! At the moment I feel like some air. Are you joining me, Eddie, or are you being the good boy and doing as the boss says?'

She avoided looking at Hugo as she spoke, but could not help hearing his swiftly indrawn breath and she tensed herself for a further attack.

To her surprise he turned on his heel and disappeared. Eddie stared after him for a few moments and then whistled softly. 'You sure ask for trouble, Tammy. I thought he was going to hit you!'

'He wouldn't dare,' she replied stoutly. 'Just because he's decided he's doing me a favour he thinks he owns me. I'll do what I want on this ship. Get me a drink, will you, Eddie, I need one right now.'

Eddie shook his head sadly as though privately deciding that she was making a big mistake, but he obediently went down below and Tammy turned to lean on the rail, looking out across the still waters of the harbour which reflected the lights from the other vessels.

Higher up on the cliff top were the lights from the town. It was a peaceful, beautiful night, but Tammy was not at peace with herself, or indeed with Hugo. War was flaring up between them and she clenched and reclenched her fists in an endeavour to control her angry thoughts.

He really thought he was master of the situation, that she would follow his bidding as meekly as did the rest of the crew. She was surprised that Eddie should be so subservient to him, for after all wouldn't it be Captain Moorbank to whom he was responsible, not Hugo Kane? Okay, it was Hugo's boat, but the Captain ran it, and when Hugo wasn't here then he was the one who issued the orders.

The more she thought about the situation the more annoyed she became, and when Eddie returned with her drink, she took a long swallow before she realised that he had brought her neat whisky.

'I thought you needed it,' he said, patting her back as she choked and spluttered on the fiery liquid. 'Something to calm down those nerves of yours.'

'I'm not nervous,' she cried hotly, 'but I'm furious! That man thinks he owns me just because we're working on his boat. Why don't we strike, teach him that we're not all meek little yes-men?'

'It wouldn't get us anywhere,' said Eddie logically. 'He'd give us the sack. Jobs on these boats are like gold. He'd have no difficulty at all in replacing us.'

'Well, I wish he'd hurry up and get somebody for my job,' she retorted crossly. 'I don't mind going any time. The trouble is he won't let me—says I'm not capable of looking after myself, and until he gets my passport back I have to stay here. He doesn't seem to be hurrying over it, though.'

Eddie smiled wryly. 'He can take as long as he likes as far as I'm concerned. You're the best thing that's happened to me in a long time.'

His arm brushed hers as they leaned against the rail and Tammy edged away because she didn't want him getting the wrong impression. 'What was Hugo doing talking to you? Where's Andrea?'

'Gone to the Casino with the Murrays and the Andersons. They asked Hugo, but he didn't want to go. Andrea wasn't very pleased. She flounced off in the end saying that she was going away, that she wasn't going to stay on this dull old boat.'

Tammy pulled a face. 'I bet he didn't like that. I should think the *Flying Queen* is his pride and joy. I've never seen such luxury except in films and glossy magazines.'

'I don't think it means all that much to him,' said Eddie, 'but it's certainly the finest ship I've ever worked on. I should hate to lose my job.'

This accounted for his deference to Hugo, decided Tammy. Perhaps he wasn't as weak as she was beginning to think, just protecting his own interests. She finished her drink, more slowly this time, and then said, 'I think I will go to bed after all. I'm feeling rather tired and if I have to be up at seven I shall need all the sleep I can get.'

'Do you have to?' wheedled Eddie, taking her glass and setting it down precariously on the handrail before pulling her into his arms. 'We've spent hardly any time together. This wasn't what I intended. I want us to get to know one another. You might even find out that you like me better than your fiancé.'

'I don't think so,' said Tammy lightly. 'I'm sorry, Eddie. I do like you, but not in that way.'

'You haven't given yourself time to find out,' he

insisted, 'and you need a friend, so why can't it be me?' His earnest face drew nearer to her own. 'Please, Tammy.'

She struggled out of his embrace. 'Friends, yes, Eddie, but anything else, no. I'm sorry, but that's the way it has to be.' The strangest part was that it was not because of David that she was saying this, and the thought disturbed her. 'Goodnight, Eddie, I'll see you in the morning.'

She went before he could say anything else, glad that the darkness hid his expression because she did not want to feel guilty at disappointing him like this.

Tammy did not hurry to her cabin; she took her time, her mind a turmoil of conflicting emotions, wondering how it could be possible to hate a man so much yet find him so deep down disturbing.

There was something about Hugo that attracted her. She wouldn't go so far as to say it was a sexual attraction, although his kiss had aroused feelings she had not known existed and which were a little bit frightening; it was more a magnetism that this type of man has for any woman, whether she likes it or not.

It was not difficult to imagine that girls would flock round him like bees round honey, and it maddened her that she was in danger of becoming one of a crowd.

'I hate him,' she told herself fiercely. 'Hate, hate, *hate!*' She must instil this into her mind so that there was never any chance of her weakening.

She frowned momentarily when she found her cabin door ajar, more or less sure that she had closed it. But she couldn't be absolutely certain, so she pushed the door open and snapped on the light, swinging it to behind her.

It was not until she turned back into the room that she saw him, sitting on the edge of her bed, his dark face as grim as ever.

For a few moments they stared at each other, cold brown eyes daring brilliant green. 'You have a nerve!' she acused. 'What are you doing here?'

'Waiting for you,' came the cutting reply. 'Isn't that obvious?'

'It is, but why?' she snapped, wondering why his presence dominated the tiny room, making her aware once again of his fatal magnetism, of the force she was striving so hard to deny.

'Because I want to talk to you and this was the only place I could think of where we wouldn't be disturbed.'

She opened the door and stood by it. 'Okay, go ahead, say what you have to say.'

'What's that for?' he asked, frowning as he nodded towards the door.

'In case I have to scream for help,' she responded drily. 'I'm afraid I don't trust you, Mr Kane.'

He pushed himself up, strode across the room and kicked the door so that it closed with an explosive bang. Then he grabbed her by the wrist and pulled her down on to the bed. As soon as she was sitting he let her go. 'That's better,' he said. 'Now, for a start, I suggest you call me Hugo and I'll call you Tammy. Perhaps with the formalities out of the way you'll be kindlier disposed towards me?'

'What's the matter?' she cried desperately. 'Jealous of Eddie? Or are you piqued because Andrea went off without you? If you're using me as second best you can forget it. You know how I feel about you.'

He smiled cruelly. 'Andrea and Marchant have nothing to do with my being here.' Lean fingers sought her arm, digging in fiercely, bruising her skin. He pulled her inexorably towards him so that she could feel his warm breath fanning her cheek and see every silver hair that streaked his dark head.

'Then what do you want?' she asked frenziedly, sitting rigid, fighting the urge to struggle because she knew that it would make no difference.

'Does there have to be a reason?' he mocked. 'Most girls I know would be delighted to have me in their room.'

Tammy was by this time slightly breathless, for no matter what she told herself the undisputed attraction was there. 'Perhaps I'm different,' she flung back, her breasts heaving. 'I don't want you here—not now, nor ever!'

Dark brows rose until they were lost in his thick thatch of hair. 'Strong sentiments. If I were you I'd be careful before saying things like that.'

She dragged her arm savagely away, using the strength of her whole body, but his grip was not broken. All she succeeded in doing was to pull him nearer towards her.

'If you think you can persuade me to change my mind you're mistaken!' she yelled. 'Let me go, you brute, before I scream loud enough for the whole ship to hear!'

'It won't get you anywhere,' he said mildly, eyes glittering with an intensity that frightened her. 'If you knew me better you'd know that I have an answer for everything. If anyone came I would soon convince them that they'd been mistaken. Besides, if they found me in your cabin they would think that you had invited me. My integrity is in too high esteem for them to believe I would force my company upon you.'

'Then they're all incredibly stupid,' flashed Tammy. 'I've never trusted you from the moment I saw you!'

'I'm not sure I agree on that,' he said slowly. 'You wouldn't have come with me if you hadn't.'

Again his compelling eyes captured her own. She stared at him defiantly. 'So—what happens next?' she rasped. 'Do I have to put up with your insufferable advances just because you happen to own this ship?'

His nostrils flared and his mouth became grim, but he controlled his feelings admirably, and when he spoke his voice was as calm and cool as though she had been doing nothing more than making pleasant conversation. 'I was hoping you'd learn to like me, Tammy,'

'For what reason?' she scoffed. 'I can't see that it matters how I feel when our association is hardly likely to be a prolonged one.'

His eyes narrowed. 'Why do you keep harping on your departure? Is life on board so intolerable?'

'The way you treat me, it is!' Her pretty face was suffused with hot colour and again she attempted to wrench herself free.

To no avail, however, for his hands slid round her waist, pulling her back on to the bed. She felt the length of his lean, hard body next to hers and heard a pounding in her ears that could only be the echo of her heart.

'Perhaps this will teach you that I'm not so terrible as you make out.' His voice came low and vibrant in her ear and the breath from his nostrils teased the fine hairs about her face.

Tammy closed her eyes, all of a sudden reluctant to look into those smouldering dark ones, to see the veiled hint of passion, the threat to her peace of mind.

When his lips found hers her limbs weakened, her heart beat erratically and everything else was forgotten. With no conscious thought her arms snaked around him, holding his body close to hers.

It was no problem for him to pull undone the tie on her dress, carefully easing the material down so that her delicately rounded breasts were exposed. With incredible gentleness he cupped one breast with his hand, caressing and teasing until Tammy's breath came in sharp bursts and a wild abandonment took the place of earlier struggles.

But it was as though her reaction triggered off controlled passion on Hugo's behalf, for his caresses became more urgent, hurting in their eagerness, his lips bruising and searing, taking what was being offered.

When his mouth sought her breasts she held his head close, arching her body, unable to help enjoying the sheer eroticism his touch evoked. It was a new and exciting experience, something she had never known could happen between two people.

When he stopped she wanted him to go on, unable to believe that he had the power to withdraw when she was enjoying herself so much. 'Hugo,' she murmured, reaching up to touch his face, to touch the dark hairs so springy and soft. 'Kiss me some more.'

The wide, triumphant smile brought her effectively back to her senses. Hugo got up from the bed and stood over her, arms akimbo. Never before had he looked so much like a pirate with his light olive skin, gleaming white teeth, and dark hair awry. The striped matelot top into which he had changed after dinner added to the effect—all he needed was a patch over one eye—and she cried out in shame.

'You see, Tammy,' he said softly, 'it's not so hard to like me, after all.'

CHAPTER FIVE

BURNING humiliation consumed Tammy as she slowly sat up, pulling her dress over her nakedness and tying it behind her neck as best she could with fingers that trembled uncontrollably. She was deeply shocked by what she had done and unable to check the shiver which took over her whole body.

'Hugo Kane,' she whispered, fighting back bitter tears. 'You're mistaken. If it's possible—I think I hate you more than ever.'

He shook his head disbelievingly, clear brown eyes still alight with success. 'You tell yourself that because you're scared to own up to the truth. Real hate would have withstood my onslaught.'

'Perhaps you underestimate your own powers,' she ripped off scornfully. 'I can't help what happened, but I do regret it, and I shall definitely make sure it doesn't happen again.'

His smile mocked her. 'We shall see. I found the whole episode highly satisfying and will certainly have no qualms about repeating the experience.'

'Your type wouldn't.' She pushed herself up and stood facing him, her hair attractively disarrayed. She swept it from her face with impatient fingers and glared hotly. 'Would you mind leaving now, *Mr Kane*?'

'I doubt you'll sleep much tonight,' he scoffed lightly. 'You'll have too much on your mind, so I may as well remain a while longer—to make sure there are no after-effects.' And he sat down resolutely on her dressing stool, smiling to himself and no doubt expecting her to object.

'Suit yourself,' she shrugged, deeply resenting this further intrusion on her privacy but equally determined not to let him see it. 'I expect you're right, as usual, I wouldn't sleep.' She sat down on the edge of the bed. 'What would you like to talk about?'

Her attitude puzzled him. Perhaps he had expected a further outburst? He frowned momentarily. 'Tell me about yourself.'

'There's not much to say,' she shrugged. 'My parents died when I was ten and I was brought up reluctantly by an aunt and uncle in Derby. As soon as I was eighteen I went to London and shared a bed-sitter with a friend. She got married and I was on my own until I met David.'

'He moved in with you?' The question was put matter-of-factly.

Tammy looked indignant. 'He did not! Neither of us approve of that sort of thing.'

'I see,' he said, though clearly not seeing at all.
'And where will you live when you're married?'

'We're moving in with his parents for a while,
until we can afford a place of our own,' and at
Hugo's look of scepticism she continued defensively,
'David's got a good job, it's just that we've set our
sights on something a little better than an ordinary
semi.'

'Sounds a solid, dependable type,' said Hugo, nodding slowly, though Tammy was not so sure that he
wasn't mocking her. 'But not your sort.'

'How would you know?' she rounded hotly. 'Besides, you've never met David, so you're in no position to judge him.'

'But I know you, my sweet little redhead, far
better than you think. You'd be bored within three
months with a man like that. I bet you never argue.
I bet life's one smooth round of visiting mother,
going to the theatre, or sitting at home while he's
away on business.'

It was so absolutely true that Tammy was shat-
tered, but that did not mean to say she was not
satisfied with the sort of life she led, or had been
leading, until this unfortunate holiday. 'I don't see
that my private life has anything to do with you,' she
said haughtily. 'What David and I do is our own
affair.'

'I agree,' he said smoothly, 'but I should hate you
to ruin your life because you're too blind to see
what's going to happen.'

At one time the prospect of such a life as Hugo
depicted had sounded a perfectly normal state of
affairs and she would have been quite content, but
he had sown a seed of doubt in her mind and now

she could not help wondering whether he spoke the truth.

Certainly her feelings had undergone a drastic change since meeting Hugo. He was so totally different from David, so masculine and virile, living such a completely different way of life. Anyone would feel dissatisfied under these circumstances, she thought angrily, but once I'm back in London things will be the same. David loves me and I love him, that's all that matters.

'Have you nothing more to say?' asked Hugo, an amused glint sparkling in his eyes. 'Perhaps I've given you food for thought? We must continue this conversation some other time, when you've had a chance to mull it over.' He rose and stretched lazily. 'Goodnight, Red, see you in the morning.'

Tammy fumed inwardly at his inference to the colour of her hair, but managed a controlled 'Goodnight, Mr Kane,' before the door closed behind him.

Once left alone she gave vent to her anger by thumping the pillows, wishing it was the man himself she was punching. He has a nerve, she raged, coming in here and telling me that I'm not marrying the right man! Who does he think he is, God?

It took her several minutes to calm sufficiently to get undressed and take a soothing shower before climbing into bed. Even so, as Hugo had predicted, sleep proved impossible, and then, just as she was dropping off Hugo's guests came back, laughing loudly, giving no thought to the fact that there might be people asleep.

When the *Flying Queen* was eventually quiet and all that could be heard was the waters of Monte Carlo harbour lapping the bottom of the boat, it was almost two. In another five hours she had to be up!

Next morning it was all Tammy could do to drag herself out of bed. She washed and dressed and made her way down to the kitchen still yawning. She was relieved to find Chips already there and a pot of coffee waiting to be drunk.

'You look as though you can do with it,' he smiled as she poured herself a cup of the steaming brown liquid and added milk and sugar.

'Gallons of the stuff,' she replied, 'to keep me awake. I had a terrible night. I hope I don't fall asleep over my job today.'

'So do I,' came Hugo's voice over her shoulder as he joined them.

She pulled a face before turning her head to give him a weak smile. 'Do your guests always make so much noise when they come back from a night out?' she asked.

'Keep you awake, did it?' he mocked. 'Funny, I never heard them, but then I fell asleep as soon as my head touched the pillow. Something on your mind, that you couldn't sleep?'

Tammy stubbornly refused to give him the satisfaction of answering, instead turning to talk to Eddie and other members of the crew who were piling into the kitchen for their breakfast.

She felt better after she had eaten and consumed another two cups of coffee. Hugo had disappeared to let them get on with their meal and she found time to clean the main saloon and the library before the guests put in an appearance for their breakfast, when she would be kept busy cleaning their staterooms.

The library was a fascinating room. As well as

hundreds of books lining the walls there were also comfortable chairs and settees in a deep green suede, with a lighter green deep-piled carpet. The daily papers were already waiting on the low tables, although the English ones, she noticed, were a day late.

She leisurely examined the books, noticing that there was something to suit all tastes, and made a mental note to come back later and find herself some suitable reading matter—if she had time! If yesterday was anything to go by her days would be filled with one round of work after another and she would fall into bed each night too exhausted to even lift a book, yet alone read it.

The main saloon was reasonably tidy, a quick polish and Hoover, the fresh flowers replaced, and it was done. She enjoyed renewing the flowers. She had a natural flair for arranging and the scope here was tremendous.

She backed towards the door to study the effect, letting out a startled, 'Oh!' when she encountered a hard, warm body behind her. Without turning she knew who it was and an electric current ran down her spine as she moved quickly away.

'Admiring your handiwork?' he asked blandly. 'They're very nice, but your time could be put to better use. My friends are already at breakfast and will expect their rooms ready when they've finished.'

Tammy took a deep breath, trying to control the rage his words induced, but even so she could not refrain from saying sarcastically, 'I'm so sorry, I must have wasted one whole minute. What are you going to do, stop it out of my wages?'

'There's no need for that,' he retorted sharply. 'I

thought I was helping you get into your routine.'

'The day you help me I'll die of shock!' she snapped. 'All you ever do is criticise. Did you follow Miss Harriet around as well, to make sure she was doing *her* work, or is it something you've reserved especially for me?'

He sighed impatiently. 'You do try a man, Tammy, and then you wonder why we're always arguing. Next time I ask you to do something perhaps you'll realise it's for your own benefit as well as mine.'

'Like hell!' she grated. 'You're used to giving orders, that's your trouble. What you don't seem to realise is that I'm different.'

'You mean you resent authority. While you're on my boat you're no different from any other crew member. You have a job of work to do and I expect it to be done thoroughly.'

'In that case,' she yelled, 'you'd better let me pass so that I can get on with it! I should hate to afford you the embarrassment of having your guests complain.'

His lips tightened grimly. 'I should have known that with hair like that you'd have a temper to match.' He stepped to one side. 'You'd better go before I do something I'll regret.'

Tammy was tempted to ask what, but decided that would be carrying things too far. It was just possible that he might carry out his threat. With her chin held high she marched outside and down the flight of steps that led to the staterooms.

The advantage of being in a temper was that Tammy got the work done extra quickly, throwing herself into the bedmaking and polishing so that when she had finished she felt exhausted. But it had the effect of cooling her exasperation and when she bumped into Hugo again as she made her way to the dining room to clear the dirty dishes she was able to greet him quite civilly.

It did surprise her, though, when he said, 'When you've finished in here you can spend a little time on the sun deck with the guests.'

In fact it was such a shock that she said acidly, 'Why? Have you had a change of heart? Have you realised that you're working me too hard?'

'Nothing of the kind,' came the short reply, and she guessed that he already regretted his impulsive offer.

'I shouldn't have said that,' she said at once. 'It's very kind of you, Mr Kane, and I appreciate your thoughtfulness.'

His grey eyes flicked over her steadily. 'I thought we'd agreed, Tammy, that it was to be Hugo. Can't you bring yourself to say my name?'

'I can,' she said huffily, 'but I don't feel we're on an equal footing, therefore I prefer to call you Mr Kane,' except in my thoughts, she added silently, you're Hugo then. Hugo the pirate who is stealing his way slowly into my heart.

'The rest of the crew call me Hugo,' he persisted, 'and I don't suppose they consider themselves my equal either, so if you wouldn't mind, let it be Hugo in future.'

She stared resentfully. 'If that's another of your well-meant orders, okay, I'll do it. But not because I want to, I must make that quite clear. To me you'll always be *Mr* Kane, my boss.'

His hand shot out as she attempted to walk past

him, her arm was caught in a crushing grip. 'Less of the sarcasm, Red,' he hissed. 'It doesn't become you.'

'It's your own fault,' she snapped, 'and don't call me Red, I don't like that either.'

'I'll call you what I like,' he said coolly. 'The name suits you better than Tamsin, which to me suggests a cold person—and you'll never be that.' He pulled her roughly towards him and kissed her, a hard, bruising kiss that took her by surprise and also released a whole gamut of emotions that she could not control.

After a few seconds he let her go. 'I won't tempt providence at this moment, but I think you know what I mean.'

Before she could think of a suitable reply he had gone. Her mouth smarted from his kiss and her heart beat erratically. She sank down on to one of the chairs, touching her lips experimentally with the tips of her fingers. If he was going to try this each time they met how could she resist him?

He was far too attractive for her peace of mind, and when she was with him all thoughts of David fled. What she couldn't understand was why he was showing an interest in her. Had he no morals? Admittedly he had said he intended finishing with Andrea, but Tammy herself had gone out of her way to tell him that she still loved David, so why the continued attention?

The more she thought about it the more confused she became, and in the end she gave up worrying and carried on with her work.

When she eventually went up on to the sun deck Hugo was absent, so too was Andrea, but both the Murrays and Andersons were reclining on loungers in their swimming gear, soaking up the wonderful Mediterranean sun.

Penny Anderson looked at Tammy as though she had no right to be there, but Margaret Murray welcomed her warmly. 'It's nice to see you putting your feet up. Hugo works you too hard considering you're only temporary. Would you like a glass of iced lemon?'

Tammy shook her head. 'I don't mind the work,' she said in defence of Hugo but without understanding why she felt it necessary to stick up for him, 'but I must agree it's nice to snatch a few minutes. Isn't the weather gorgeous? I doubt they've got anything like this in England.'

'Nor Scotland,' said Maggie ruefully. 'Have you ever been to our part of the country, Tammy?' and as the girl shook her head, 'I'll give you our address and you must promise to visit us some time.'

'I'd love that,' said Tammy, thinking what a nice person Mrs Murray was. Her husband, Tom, was quietly immersed in a newspaper, so too was Keith Anderson, but Penny now joined in the conversation.

'Of course, that's why we moved to Monaco, because of the weather. It's so ghastly in England, I don't know how I stood it.'

'It's what we get used to,' said Maggie. 'Is this your first time abroad, Tammy?'

But before she could answer Penny butted in, 'Of course it is, didn't you know? She was supposed to be on honeymoon but her boy-friend called the wedding off. Why was that, Tammy, I never did find out?'

Tammy felt like telling her to mind her own business, but for the sake of convention she answered evenly, 'His business took him away. The wedding's only postponed, not cancelled altogether, in case you were wondering.'

Penny gave a disbelieving smile. 'So he tells you, but it sounds highly suspicious to me. I should watch him, if I were you. I wouldn't be surprised if he has some other girl in mind and this is his way of letting you down gently.'

'Don't be horrid,' interjected Maggie quickly. 'I'm sure it's nothing like that. Tammy's a lovely girl, why should he want anyone else?'

'Men are strange creatures,' replied Penny. 'Take Hugo, for instance. We all thought at one time he was going to marry Andrea, but he's certainly cooled towards her recently.'

'I haven't noticed anything,' said Mrs Murray, 'and they've gone off together now.'

'Only because she asked him,' returned Penny darkly. 'I mean, he wouldn't go to the Casino last night, and that's not Hugo.'

Tammy said, 'Is he a gambling man?' But as soon as she had asked the question she knew it was stupid. After all, hadn't she met him at Emil Conin's casino? Admittedly he wasn't playing, but he wouldn't have been there if he had not intended to play, surely?

'He enjoys a game,' answered Mrs Murray, 'but I'll say this for him, he knows when to stop. Not like some people I know.'

Her eyes flickered towards the Andersons as she spoke, but they were too thick-skinned to realise she was referring to them. Penny waved a hand airily towards Tammy. 'Fetch me a lager and lime, there's a dear. I could do with a long, cool drink.'

'There's lemon here,' said Maggie. 'Let the poor girl rest, she deserves it.'

But Penny Anderson answered peremptorily, 'I want a lager. You know I never drink that stuff.'

Rather than cause an argument between the two women Tammy jumped to her feet. 'I'll fetch you one this time, Mrs Anderson,' she said with dignity, 'but I must remind you that serving drinks is not one of my jobs.'

'Oh, really,' cooed Penny. 'I thought you were here to do anything. General dogsbody, that's what Andrea told me.'

'Maybe she did,' said Tammy lightly, 'but it's not true.'

'I have only your word for that,' replied Penny nastily. 'You're trying to shirk your work, if you ask me. And why are you sitting down now? It's not normal for the crew to mingle with the guests, not socially. You're here to look after us, not join us.'

Tammy was furious. This woman really was the limit! She said coldly, 'I'm sorry, Mrs Anderson, but I don't see myself as any different from you. The only difference is I'm working for my money and yours fell into your lap. All I can say is that I hope I never win the pools if it turns me into a snob like you!'

Penny shot to her feet and if Maggie hadn't pulled her back Tammy was sure she would have struck her. It was easy to tell the woman had no breeding, and in some strange way she felt sorry for her.

'You haven't heard the last of this!' yelled Penny angrily.

'I don't suppose I have,' agreed Tammy, her calm

acceptance infuriating the other woman further. But she did not stay to hear any more, instead making her way down to the sanctity of the kitchen and the comforting Chips.

'Have you any coffee on?' she asked. 'I've just had a go with Penny Anderson and I could do with some sustenance.'

'You're not on your own,' he said solicitously. 'Eddie was in earlier, she's been ordering him around as though he was dirt, and when he could take no more and answered her back she said she was going to report him to the Captain.'

Tammy pulled a wry face. 'That makes two of us. Why does Mr Kane put up with her? I don't see how he can call her a friend.'

'It's Keith Anderson who's really Hugo's friend,' explained the chef. 'He did him a good turn once and this is Hugo's way of repaying him.'

'Giving them free holidays when they've got piles of money like that? The man's insane!'

'Soft-hearted,' amended Chips. 'He doesn't look it. Anyone who doesn't know would think he was a cold, ruthless character—but he's not, I can assure you of that.'

Tammy would have liked to disagree, but she had not come down to start another argument and gratefully accepted the coffee Chips handed to her.

Ten minutes later she felt better and as there was another half hour before she need start work again she shut herself in the library, eagerly scanning the titles for something that appealed.

There were the complete works of Shakespeare, Dickens, Tolstoy, Thomas Hardy, as well as a vast number of unknown authors, all looking as though they were well read. In the end she selected a romantic thriller and curled herself up one one of the suede-covered chairs.

Soon she had become so immersed that she forgot the time. It was not until the door burst open and Hugo appeared, his face suffused by dark anger, that she glanced at her watch.

Anxiously she scrambled to her feet. 'I'm sorry,' she began. 'I—I was reading, I didn't realise it was so late.'

'That's not why I'm here,' said Hugo, 'but since you mention it—yes, what are you doing sitting reading when you should be working?'

'You told me I could take some time off,' said Tammy defensively.

He glanced at his own watch. 'It's now almost one. How long have you been here?'

She shrugged. 'Since about eleven, I suppose. I said I was sorry, I'll go and do the table now.'

'Wait!' he barked, holding up his hand. 'I've had a complaint from Mrs Anderson. What have you been saying to her?'

'Only what she deserved,' Tammy answered hotly, her green eyes wide and hostile. 'She started it, but I don't suppose she told you that. I expect she only gave you her side of the story.'

'Penny is my guest,' said Hugo coldly. 'As such she is entitled to civility from the crew.'

'And we're expected to take what she gives? Eddie had the same trouble with her—has she told you about him as well?'

'At this precise moment,' he informed her coldly, 'it's you we're discussing. Perhaps it was a bad error of judgment on my behalf, believing you could mix easily with them, but this doesn't condone your behaviour. In future, Miss Swift, I would ask you to curb your tongue.'

So it was back to Miss Swift! So much for thinking he might be attracted towards her, but in a way it helped, because it effectively stopped her from getting any ideas about him.

She tossed her head arrogantly. 'If you think I'll have insults slung at me and do nothing about it, you're mistaken! Don't you know me better than that? As you once so accurately pointed out, I don't have red hair for nothing.'

'The way I heard it,' he said grimly, 'it was Penny who had the insults hurled at her.'

'Only because she provoked me,' shouted Tammy. 'I don't suppose she told you about that? General dogsbody, that's what she called me, but I'm not, and you know it, and you'd better put her right before she starts me off again!'

Tammy had never been so angry in her life, and before she could stop herself she was pounding her fists on his chest, trying to hammer home her words.

Hugo remained unmoved and let her get on with it, looking down at her with those thick-fringed dark eyes, which at this moment were quite coldly angry. 'If you've finished,' he said at length, 'I suggest you run along and get on with your work.'

'Not until you promise to tell Mrs Anderson I'm not her slave,' she said frigidly, her hands falling now to her sides, but still with the light of battle in her eyes.

He frowned, his thick brows beetling together. 'Perhaps you're not familiar yet with the running of the *Flying Queen*? My friends expect, and indeed usually get, personalised service—that's one of the nicest things about holidays on this class of boat. Guests are taken care of at all times. Pampered, spoilt if you like, they have only to lift their finger to demand whatever they like.'

'And is that the sort of life *you* lead?' scoffed Tammy. 'Is your house run with a retinue of servants who hasten to do your slightest bidding?'

'That will do, Tammy,' he rasped harshly, dropping his hands heavily on her shoulders. 'You're getting carried away, and I wouldn't advise that.'

'What do you suggest?' she asked fiercely, 'that I go and apologise to Penny Anderson? Because I won't. You can throw me off for all I care, but I'll never say I'm sorry to that woman, not in a hundred years, and you can tell her from me that if she messes up her cabin again after I've done it, she'll have to do it herself!'

'You'll do as you're told,' said Hugo softly, threateningly, the pressure of his fingers increasing slightly to add emphasis to his words. 'And I would request that before you go into the dining room you control that temper of yours.'

'I can't help it,' she muttered mutinously, 'when everyone insists on treating me like a slave.'

'I presume by *everyone* you mean Penny and myself?' he asked slowly.

'So far,' she ground out bitterly, 'but I wouldn't put it past Andrea to try it on as well. It was she who told Mrs Anderson that I was a general dogsbody.'

His lips quirked this time. 'Not a very flattering description, I must admit. I can certainly think of far better ones. But it's right to a certain degree. I did explain how arduous the job was.'

'But you didn't give me the chance to turn it down,' she cried defensively, wriggling free from his grasp and rubbing her shoulders. 'Perhaps you think I should be grateful that I have a roof over my head, but I'm beginning to think I would have been better off fending for myself.'

Hugo sighed deeply and impatiently. 'You're not a prisoner, Tammy. I'm only concerned for your well-being, but if staying here distresses you so much you're free to go.' He turned away, as though dismissing her from his mind.

Tammy was tempted to say there and then that she would go, but she realised that she would be a fool to do so. Besides, she had no money, unless she asked Hugo for some. The thought was distasteful.

'There's not much point,' she said dispiritedly.

'In that case,' came the terse reply, 'you'd better go and lay the table before I get some more complaints.'

CHAPTER SIX

DESPITE the fact that Tammy tried to push her argument with Penny Anderson to the back of her mind, she could not help the resentment which built up inside her every time she was forced to serve her at lunch.

With Hugo's eagle eye upon her it made matters worse, and when the woman pushed her plate of Chicken Maryland away, saying it was cold, Tammy felt like tipping the contents over her head. No one else had complained and she guessed that Penny was doing it to be awkward.

Nevertheless she had no alternative but to take the food back to Chips, who let out a string of oaths which surprised Tammy. 'If he dares invite that woman another year I shall leave,' he said adamantly. 'There's no call for such high-handed behaviour. The chicken wasn't cold. You know the fuss I make about serving food hot. Take it back as it is, Tammy, let's see what she says then. I've a sneaking suspicion she won't dare complain a second time.'

And she didn't. When Tammy put the plate back in front of her the woman ate her meal with no fuss whatsoever, although she did change her mind about the sweet after Tammy had served it, and Tammy could not resist banging the plate down in front of her with her second choice.

She refused to look at Hugo, pretty sure he must be frowning with annoyance. Let him! she thought hotly. I'm doing the best I can. Any minute now I shall explode and Mrs Anderson really will have a plate of food over her head!

The thought amused her and she could not help smiling. At the same time she caught Hugo's eye and he gave her a brief nod back, as though reassured that she had come out of her temper and was giving his approval. If only he knew why she was smiling!

When they had finished and Tammy had once again straightened the dining room and eaten her own lunch, there was little left to do until it was time for the evening meal.

Several times Tammy had walked past the beauty salon that was installed in the ship, but she had said no more than a casual hello to the woman who ran it. Now she decided to pay her a visit and was greeted enthusiastically by the manageress who introduced herself as Karina.

'I'm glad to meet you at last,' she said. 'I've wanted to talk to you, but you always seem so busy. Lost your passport, I hear, and Hugo's taken you in until it's found?'

Tammy nodded, immediately liking this plump, friendly woman, who looked nothing like a beauty specialist.

'Hugo's a good man,' continued Karina. 'He has a heart of gold.'

'Really!' said Tammy acidly.

The older woman looked surprised. 'You don't get on with him? I can't believe that, Tammy, Hugo gets on with everyone.'

'Then he's singled me out,' Tammy declared, 'but I haven't come here to discuss Mr Kane,' realising that she was being disloyal and that for all she knew Karina might relay their conversation and then she would be in trouble again, 'I want to know if you can do anything with my hair. The sea air's playing havoc with it.'

Karina chatted incessantly as she washed and set Tammy's hair, saying how much she enjoyed her job and could never see herself working anywhere else. 'I don't open every day,' she said, 'not with only three women on board—four including yourself, of course,' she added as an afterthought. 'Sometimes, when the boat's chartered out to strangers, there's a whole crowd of people and I'm kept so busy I have to take on extra help. I prefer it like this, then I can spend time visiting my married sister in San Remo.'

'Are you married?' asked Tammy. Karina looked

as though she was in her late forties, yet she wore no ring.

'I was once,' she admitted, 'but it was a mistake, and I don't intend making another one. I'm quite happy as I am, and I certainly shouldn't like to go back to England.'

'It is nice here,' agreed Tammy, 'but I haven't really had much time to look around. The weather's gorgeous, though, even if I don't have much time to enjoy it.'

'It's a hard job, yours,' concurred Karina as she put the last roller into Tammy's hair and positioned her beneath the dryer. 'I shouldn't like it. It's all right, of course, when you get a good crowd on board, but when you get someone as unpleasant as Penny Anderson—well, it makes the job that much more difficult.'

'She plays you up too?' asked Tammy.

Karina nodded emphatically. 'But I get my own back,' she laughed. 'I don't know why, but she always gets shampoo in her eyes, and I manage to forget her when she's under the dryer.'

Tammy giggled appreciatively. 'So long as you don't forget me.'

'You—I like,' said Karina. 'Would you like me to do your nails while you're under there?'

Since the treatment was costing her nothing Tammy agreed. It was nice to be pampered and her hands had certainly suffered in the two days she had worked here.

When she finally emerged from the salon several hours later—Karina having kept up a voluble stream of conversation that made getting away difficult—Tammy felt like a new woman. Karina had

arranged her hair in a completely different style
with soft curls framing her face while the rest was
taken up out of her neck. 'It's too hot to wear it
loose,' advised Karina. 'If you can't manage it yourself pop in any time and I'll fix it. You have beautiful hair and such a lovely colour. You don't often see
that precise shade of auburn.'

This pleased Tammy, following Hugo's reference
to it as red, and there was quite a spring to her step
as she made her way down to her cabin ready to
change for the evening meal. She might be a cleaner,
she told herself, but she certainly had no intention
of looking like one!

She chose a dress in soft, misty blue and made up
her face with more care than usual, feeling that her
new hairstyle deserved complementary treatment.

As she emerged from her cabin she saw Hugo
coming towards her. Closing her door quickly, she
began to walk along the corridor to meet him.

'You want me?' she asked pleasantly, tilting her
chin in order to look up at him, her emerald eyes
sparkling with a glint of humour. She felt good at
the moment, confident that nothing he could say
would upset her.

He appraised her slowly, keen eyes missing not
one detail of her elegant appearance. 'Is that an
offer?' he mocked, 'if so, I'll certainly take you up on
it.'

'It is not an offer, and you know very well what
I mean,' said Tammy coolly, even though her heart
jumped wildly at the thought of being taken yet
again into those powerful arms and pressed against
the hard strength of his masculinity.

He leaned arrogantly against the wall, his arms

folded as he continued to survey her. 'You look ex-
tremely charming, Tammy, if I may be permitted to
say so. I'm almost sorry I'm going out tonight.'

Tammy was too. Her excitement took a sudden
downward plunge. She had not realised that she had
dressed up for Hugo's benefit, but now it became
immediately obvious to her, and she despised herself
for it. She professed to hate the man yet had sub-
consciously gone out of her way to attract him. What
a contrary creature she was becoming!

'Was that what you wanted to tell me, that you're
going out tonight?' she asked distantly.

He nodded. 'We're all going, so don't wait up.
You need your sleep—after last night.'

She wouldn't have waited anyway, but if they
made as much noise coming back as they had before
then she wouldn't sleep again. If this sort of thing
went on every night by the end of a week she would
be completely exhausted.

'Thank you for telling me,' she said politely. 'I
hope you have a good time. Where are you going?'

Hugo shrugged. 'We're taking a ride into Nice.
Who knows, I may come upon your friend Emil.'

Tammy looked at him sharply, not sure whether
he meant he was going to seek him out deliberately,
or whether he meant what he said, and that their
meeting could be purely accidental. She said hope-
fully, 'I do hope so. I'm beginning to think I shall
never get my things back.'

Hugo shoved his hands into his pockets, obviously
in no hurry to finish their conversation. 'You sound
eager to be gone.'

'You already know that,' she said scathingly.

'If circumstances were different,' he probed, 'let's

say you were spending a holiday on my boat, not working, would you enjoy it then, or does this way of life not appeal to you at all?'

Tammy thought for a moment. Up until now she had never really considered the question as there was not the remotest chance that she could afford a holiday of this sort. But, hypothetically speaking, she supposed it would be enjoyable. To be waited on at all times, to enjoy only the best in food and surroundings—it would be the experience of a life-time.

She nodded slowly. 'I expect I would, I'd be a fool not to, but I don't see any sense in thinking about it when it's not likely to happen to me.'

Her reply drew a satisfied smile from her companion. 'It was the answer I was expecting. Now, I won't detain you any longer, I expect you have work to do.'

His reaction puzzled her and she wondered why he had asked her in the first place. Certainly not because he had any real interest. He knew it was absolutely out of the question for her to even contemplate such a holiday. Idle curiosity perhaps?

She shrugged as she made her way up the two lots of stairs, setting the table automatically, scarcely thinking what she was doing.

Andrea gave her a long, haughty stare when she came in a half hour later, only Maggie commenting on her new hairstyle. Hugo ignored her altogether and she wondered whether he was afraid of upsetting Andrea if he paid too much attention to his latest employee.

Not that she could see Hugo being afraid of anyone or anything, but it could undoubtedly cause unpleasantness and as Andrea was a guest on his ship she supposed he felt it advisable to keep the peace.

This time they did not linger over their meal and in a remarkably short space of time the table was cleared and Tammy was enjoying her own dinner.

The crew normally had to eat in relays so that there was always someone on hand to look after the guests, but tonight they were all together and Tammy found herself relaxing in their convivial company.

Even the Captain, with whom she had had scarcely any contact, gave her a considerable amount of his attention, and she found herself quite liking him, in spite of the fact that in the beginning she had thought him as hard a man as Hugo.

He told her about his wife and children who lived in Marseilles. 'They don't really like me being away from home for such long spells, but the money is good, so——' He shrugged vaguely.

'Is your wife French?' asked Tammy.

Captain Moorbank shook his head. 'No, she's English, but she chose to live in Marseilles so that I can easily go home when I have time off.'

'I've noticed that all the crew are English,' said Tammy. 'Why's that, doesn't Mr Kane trust foreigners?'

He laughed. 'It's not that. He believes in being loyal to his fellow countrymen, that's all. Can't say I blame him.'

Shortly after that Eddie claimed her attention, suggesting that when their meal was finished they spend the evening together.

Why not? thought Tammy. Why should she do as Hugo Kane said? She deserved a little pleasurable relaxation, and the company of Eddie was just what she needed.

Karina nudged her elbow as she left the room, having heard Eddie issue his invitation. 'Keep your eye on that one,' she advised, 'he can prove quite a handful at times.'

Tammy laughed, 'Are you speaking from experience?'

But the hairdresser merely smiled knowingly and went on her way. Although Karina was older than Eddie, Tammy would not put it past him to have made a pass at her. She imagined that women were his life blood and without their company he would find the days incredibly dull. She felt capable of handling him, though, and looked forward to an hour or so in his company, safe in the knowledge that Hugo would not be interrupting them.

For the first half hour they went up on deck, looking out across the serene stillness of the harbour, at the rising heights of Monte Carlo on their one side and the Palace of Monaco on the other. Eddie's arm was about her waist as they leaned against the rail and Tammy did not resist. In fact it felt comforting to have the undivided attention of this man, even though she knew that her feelings would not go any further than simple friendship.

Eddie had other ideas, she knew that, but if she didn't encourage him perhaps in time he would realise that her love lay elsewhere.

Thinking about David made her remember that she still had not posted her letter. It was in her bag where she had placed it as soon as she had written, thinking that the next time she went ashore she would post it. But she had not left the boat since. Perhaps Eddie would post it for her, or preferably the Murrays, who would be more reliable. She would ask them first thing in the morning.

'You haven't listened to a word I've been saying,' grumbled Eddie goodnaturedly as he gave her a gentle shake. 'Where were you?'

'I was thinking about David,' she admitted truthfully.

'Wondering what he would say if he saw us together?' Eddie grinned. 'It's his bad luck for letting you go. If a fellow's fool enough to let his girl go wandering round France on her own then he has to take the consequences.'

'He didn't want me to,' protested Tammy, feeling that she had to put things straight. 'In fact he was furious.'

'Yet you still came? Didn't his feelings matter?'

They should have, thought Tammy. Strange how she could see this now, when she was hundreds of miles away from him, yet she hadn't at the time! Did it mean that even then she had not loved him as much as she had professed? Admittedly since they had been apart she had thought of him less and less, and only she knew that Hugo had had a lot to do with it.

'I was too angry at the time to care how he felt,' she answered at last. 'I couldn't believe that he would put business before me, before our wedding. How would you like it?'

'I wouldn't,' said Eddie firmly, his arm tightening about her waist. 'I think it's an insult and I regard it as my duty to keep you happy while you're here. He doesn't deserve such a wonderful girl as you.'

'Flatterer!' she laughed, feeling a tiny bit guilty discussing David like this. She loved him really, *she did!* Or at least that was what she kept trying to convince herself.

As dusk fell the air got cooler and when Tammy gave an involuntary shiver Eddie insisted that they move inside.

The main saloon was deserted. Tammy sat on one of the comfortable leather armchairs while Eddie poured her a drink from the cocktail bar whose lid opened automatically at the touch of a button.

When he came and perched himself on the arm of her chair, she felt dismayed. She had purposely chosen this seat so that he would have to sit elsewhere, and now here he was, his arm resting lightly across her shoulders, the lights dimmed intimately and a cassette sending sweet, seductive music into the room.

She jumped to her feet. 'Let's see what's on television,' she said brightly. 'I haven't seen any since I left England.'

The fact that they had television at all on the *Flying Queen* amazed her, but Hugo had explained that all the main services, water, electricity, telephone, television, were connected. Living on the boat was in fact no different from living in a house. 'It's what we pay for,' he had said matter-of-factly. 'Some of the boats even have a telex system installed so that they can keep in touch with their business activities.'

Eddie did not look too pleased at the fact that Tammy preferred to watch television. He no doubt thought that his company should be sufficient. It would have been had she not guessed what was in his mind and she had no intention of allowing him to become too intimate.

Unfortunately the picture that sprang on to the

screen was of a naked couple in bed, and although the dialogue was in French, Tammy had no difficulty in understanding the situation.

Eddie laughed at her embarrassment and she turned it off quickly. 'Mr Kane says he has some video tapes somewhere. Do you know where they are? I enjoy a good Western and he assured me he had plenty of those.'

'Isn't my company good enough?' asked Eddie sulkily. 'We don't need to have entertainment provided for us, surely?'

Tammy gave him a rueful grin, not daring to say that she was trying to avoid the amorous advances she was sure he would make later. 'I thought it would make a change,' she explained. 'I find television so relaxing.'

He put down his drink, started the tape again, and came across the room. 'You can relax with me,' he said softly, kissing her lips in a light, friendly manner.

Afterwards he pulled her down on to the settee and they sat quietly together in complete harmony, the light, pleasant music soothing so that when Tammy found herself drawn into Eddie's arms she had no desire to resist.

'My beautiful Tammy,' he whispered, 'you're quite the nicest thing that's happened to me this summer.'

'I don't believe you,' she smiled, 'but it's a nice thought all the same, thank you.' And when he attempted to kiss her she thought it would be churlish to refuse after his compliment, so she gave her lips freely, and in fact quite enjoyed his embrace.

It was not until he began to get carried away that

Tammy resisted. 'No, Eddie,' she cried, 'you know I don't feel for you in that way.'

'Oh, come off it,' he slurred. 'You're enjoying this as much as me,' and he clamped his lips on hers yet again.

So intense had he become that it frightened Tammy and she pushed against him with all her strength. But to no avail. His arms held her like bands of steel and his hot lips pursued every inch of her face and neck.

When he attempted to slip her dress from her shoulders Tammy renewed her struggles, but Eddie's strength was greater than hers and he laughed, far too emotionally involved to care whether his partner was responding or not.

But when, despite her struggles, he managed to manoeuvre her dress off her shoulders, revealing the lovely nakedness of her breasts, Tammy really saw red, and as he lowered his head to kiss her she sank her own teeth into the back of his neck.

Eddie swore angrily, eyes blazing with uncontrollable passion. 'You want to play rough?' he queried, 'well, that's all right with me,' and before she even had any idea of what he was going to do he had torn the dress from her completely and was bearing down on top of her.

Her heart beat painfully, echoing like jungle drums in her ears. She closed her eyes both against Eddie and the flood of angry tears that threatened, realising that she had let herself in for this. She should never have encouraged him in the first place, she ought to have realised what sort of a man he was. Hugo had warned her, but she hadn't listened, not really believing that Eddie would go this far. A mild flirtation she hadn't minded, but now——?

She opened her eyes wide and all she could see were Eddie's triumphant brown ones as he lowered himself down on her.

'Please, Eddie,' she pleaded, 'please——'

But she got no further, her cries were drowned beneath the harsh, resonant tones of Hugo's furious voice. Neither had heard him come into the room, but they both heard him now.

'Marchant, I know I have no control over you carrying on your affairs, but please, not in the main saloon. Use your cabin if you wish to continue such disgusting behaviour.'

Eddie shot up as though a gun was at his head and backed awkwardly across the room. 'I wasn't expecting you yet, Hugo.'

'Obviously,' came the biting retort. 'Get out, before I kick you out. Miss Swift will join you later, if she's still willing. Somehow I doubt she will be after I've finished with her.'

Tammy swivelled her eyes up at the taut figure in the centre of the room. He bristled with anger and his eyes were as coldly furious as she had ever seen them.

She looked away quickly, expecting Eddie to come to her defence, to say that she had not been a willing partner and that it was all his fault.

When he said nothing, when he walked meekly out without another word, she was so shocked she could say nothing. The tears that had threatened before sprang to the surface, the injustice of the situation searing through her like a flame.

She felt sickened and averted her face. It had to be her fault as well as Eddie's, even if her encouragement had been no more than a friendly gesture to another crew member who was lonely like herself.

She should have known better than to think that Eddie could be trusted, after all the warnings she had been given. But she had thought him harmless enough. She had known he was a flirt, but she had never thought he would go this far.

Pulling herself into a sitting position, Tammy tucked her feet beneath her and covered as much of herself as possible with her hands, then she looked at Hugo, determined that he should speak first. If she said anything he would think she was trying to make excuses. He would never believe that she hadn't encouraged the chief steward.

His cold, condemning eyes scoured her body insultingly and Tammy felt this more embarrassing than Eddie seeing her naked, for he had been too eager to possess her to take the time to look at her as Hugo did now.

'Emil Conin clearly assessed your character better than me,' he grated, his voice harsh with suppressed emotion. 'I should have let you stay and take the consequences.'

Forgetting her modesty, Tammy sprang to her feet. 'If you think I let Eddie willingly——'

But she got no further. Hugo silenced her with his hand. 'I want no explanations or excuses. I saw and heard enough to draw my own conclusions.' His eyes flicked her body scornfully now, his breathing deepened and nostrils flared.

His fists at his sides clenched until she could see the white of his knuckles and the censure in his eyes was like a whiplash. She cringed, but stood her ground. 'I might have known you'd condemn me!

You've had it in for me ever since we met. What I want to know is why you bothered in the first place?'

'Because I thought you worthy of a better life than the one Conin was offering,' he rasped. 'Seems like I was mistaken and that your body is for sale after all, whether it's for money or pure good gold sexism.'

Tammy's hand shot out and met the inflexible hardness of his cheek. 'How dare you! *How dare you!* I hate you, Hugo Kane, and I'm leaving this ship right now!'

A curious smile flickered about the corners of his mouth. 'I'll help you,' and in an instant he had swung her up into his arms and was carrying her out of the saloon. She kicked and struggled and shouted in vain as Hugo made his way up the short flight of steps to the deck, and scarcely before she knew what was happening she was standing on the quayside and Hugo had disappeared back on board the *Flying Queen*.

Grateful for the darkness which hid both her blushes and her semi-nudeness, Tammy glanced warily about her, relieved to see that there was no one about. She had never in her life been so angry as she was at this moment. Humiliation took second place. Hugo had treated her with no more compunction than he would a stray cat, dumping her down and more or less saying, 'Here, fend for yourself in future.'

The sound of voices a couple of hundred yards away galvanised her into action. It was either their own party returning or people from the other boats. In either case she did not, could not, be seen like

this, and she scurried back on board, mentally crossing her fingers that she would bump into no one
until she reached the safety of her cabin.

She closed the door behind her and not even
bothering to put on the light threw herself down on
to the bed, giving a shriek of pure terror when her
hands encountered the warm hardness of another
body.

It was either Eddie, wanting to finish off what he
had started, or Hugo, ready to throw her out yet
again. She backed across the room and flicked the
switch, not knowing whether to be relieved or in-
timidated that it was the grim dark face of her
employer that faced her.

He smiled with his lips only, his eyes like two
chips of ice perpetually frozen. 'I thought you might
come back,' he said, and his voice held not an atom
of emotion, it was as cold and distant as his eyes.

'What did you expect me to do?' she yelled, 'run
around Monte Carlo like this?'

'You wouldn't have been alone for long,' he returned levelly. 'That is what you want, I presume,
male company?'

Why bother to deny it when he had clearly made
up his mind as to the type of girl she was? She
shrugged and grabbed her nylon negligee which
hung on the back of the door.

'Oh no, you don't.' Hugo got up and plucked the
white garment from her fingers. 'I prefer you as you
are. You obviously had no qualms about Eddie seeing you, so why should I be any different?'

His eyes raked her body insolently, lingering on
her perfectly shaped breasts until Tammy felt her

stomach tying itself in knots and her pulses raced
erratically.

She crossed her arms in front of her, but he pulled
them away, holding them down at her sides while
he continued his slow, deliberate exploration.

When she could stand no more Tammy snapped,
'I'm surprised you can bear to touch me, Mr Kane,
if I'm the type of girl you're insinuating. Or do you
like that sort? Is that why you were at Emil Conin's
casino, hoping to pick yourself up a pretty young
girl who would keep you entertained for the evening?'

This time it was he who slapped her, and she
reeled back, touching her burning cheek, staring at
him incredulously with wide, very green eyes.

'I'm not going to apologise,' Hugo said instantly,
'even though I've never done that sort of thing before, and I hope I won't be goaded into doing it
again, but if anyone tries me it's you, Tammy Swift.
For God's sake get dressed before you torture a man
to death!'

He snatched open her wardrobe door and pulled
out the first dress he came to, flinging it savagely
across the room.

Tammy caught it and dragged it swiftly over her
head. It was all she could do to stand up, her limbs
were trembling so violently. Hugo must have
noticed, but he did not invite her to sit, even though
he had resumed his seat on the bed.

'One more episode like that, Tammy, and I won't
be responsible for my actions. I wish to God now
I'd seen Conin tonight. I don't want you on my ship
any longer.'

CHAPTER SEVEN

TAMMY stared helplessly at Hugo. Her cheek still stung from his slap, but surprisingly she did not hate him for it. She had not meant what she said and had deserved his reprimand, even though it had come as something of a shock.

What did hurt was the fact that he had said he no longer wanted her on board the *Flying Queen*. Not until this moment had she realised the true state of her feelings for Hugo.

She loved him!

A helpless, searing love, about which she could do nothing. There had been a time when he had expressed a wish to become more friendly, and she had spurned him. Now there was no chance, none at all, and all because of her stupidity in encouraging Eddie.

'I'm sorry,' she whispered meekly, not really knowing what else to say.

'Sorry!' he echoed loudly, 'for what, carrying on an affair with my chief steward? Your apology makes no difference to the way I feel. The unfortunate part is I'm stuck with you for the moment whether I like it or not. Just make sure you keep out of my way. First thing tomorrow I'll seek out Conin and get your damn passport back one way or another.'

'You won't cause any trouble?' Tammy was concerned now for Hugo's safety. She didn't want him getting involved in any fights on her behalf.

Hugo sneered, 'Don't worry, I won't lay a finger on your friend Conin. Threats are enough to frighten that man into action.'

He's not my friend, Tammy wanted to cry out, but what was the use? Hugo had it firmly fixed into his mind now that she was of easy virtue, and to argue to the contrary would only make matters worse. In fact it would be a relief to return to England, even though it would break her heart never to see Hugo again.

Voices were heard now above them—the others had returned. Hugo got to his feet and moved swiftly across the room. The door whistled behind him and she heard his footsteps marching angrily along the corridor.

Even then she did not move. Leaning back against the wall, she covered her face with her hands, allowing bitter tears to fall unchecked. Slowly she slid down until she was sitting on the floor and there she sobbed until sheer exhaustion made her stop.

With arms and legs that felt as though they were weighted by lead she dragged off her clothes and slipped into a nightdress, and without bothering to wash flung herself down on top of the bed.

There she slept, waking in the middle of the night shivering and crawling between the sheets to sleep again, the toll of the last two exhausting days taking their effect.

When morning came she found that she had overslept and already voices and movements could be heard all around her. Hurriedly she showered and dressed, forgoing any make-up and doing nothing but drag a brush through her hair, her beautiful new hairdo of yesterday completely ruined.

To her surprise the dining table was already set and when she went into the kitchen Chips and Eddie were talking quietly together. 'Good morning,' she called, in a voice far more cheerful than she was feeling.

Eddie turned swiftly and came across to her, taking her by the elbows and looking deep into her eyes. 'Tammy, can you ever forgive me? I guess I was drunk with passion and didn't know what I was doing.'

Tammy shook her head helplessly. 'Forget it, Eddie.' That was what she was trying to do. She had determinedly thrust the whole episode from her mind this morning—otherwise she would end up in tears again—and not for anything would she let Hugo know she was upset. 'It's over and done with so far as I'm concerned and I don't want to discuss it again.'

'Does that mean I've completely blotted my copy-book? That I've spoilt whatever chance I had with you?' asked Eddie anxiously.

'You never did stand a chance,' Tammy replied patiently, 'there's David, don't forget.' But relenting slightly, 'Perhaps I shouldn't have encouraged you, it's my fault as much as yours. Don't look so sad, we can still be friends—but that's all.'

A smile chased the shadows from his face and he looked once again the carefree man she had first met. 'Thanks, Tammy, I promise I won't pester you again—at least, I'll try not to.'

She was compelled to return his smile. 'Okay, Eddie, but there's work to be done. What kind person laid the table for me?'

Chips, who had been pretending not to listen to

their conversation, turned their way. 'Eddie did, on my instructions. I guessed you'd overslept.' He winked solemnly. 'Can't let my favourite girl get into trouble!'

He really was a dear, thought Tammy, as she moved out of the kitchen to put the final touches to the table. If only Eddie would be satisfied with a platonic friendship as well, then she would have no worries.

But for Eddie to remain just good friends with a girl was asking the impossible, she knew that, and despite his promise she knew she would still have to watch him carefully if she did not want a repeat of last night's episode.

It was a relief not to have to serve at breakfast. Tammy could not have stood facing Hugo this morning. She waited until they were all eating and then moved swiftly downstairs to begin her work on the cabins.

As she straightened Hugo's sheets a feeling of tenderness came over her, and she knew that no matter how he treated her it would make no difference to the love that was growing in her heart. At this precise moment she did not feel guilty about David. She loved Hugo, and that thought clouded her vision to all else.

Almost without thinking she lay down on his bed and tried to imagine what it would be like with him beside her. She closed her eyes, surprised by the intensity of her emotions. There was a faint lingering odour on the pillow which teased her nostrils and caused her breathing to deepen as though she had taken some violent physical exercise.

Without any warning the door opened and Hugo

appeared, coming to an abrupt halt when he saw
Tammy lying on his bed. First he frowned and then
he smiled, wickedly, menacingly. 'An open invitation, no less! My luck must be in.'

Before she could even think about moving he had
kicked off his shoes and was on the bed, kneeling
over her, pinning her down so that escape was impossible.

'To what do I owe this honour?' he asked
grimly, his smile now gone.

'Go to hell!' she snapped, turning her head and
refusing to look at him.

'There must be some explanation,' he insisted,
gripping her chin between thumb and forefinger
and twisting her head painfully round so that she
was forced to meet his eyes. 'And don't tell me you
were tired, because that won't wash. I happen to
know that you were late getting up this morning. It
surprises me that you managed to sleep at all—but
then I suppose a girl like you has no conscience.'

Tammy looked at him stonily, refusing to be
goaded, instead wondering how she could possibly
love a man who treated her so despicably.

'You're not going to tell me?' A gloating smile
appeared in those dark eyes. 'Then I shall be forced
to draw my own conclusions, though it does puzzle
me as to how you knew I'd be back before I'd
finished my breakfast.'

Again Tammy remained stubbornly silent.

'But it doesn't matter, does it? What is important
is that you're here, apparently offering yourself to
me. Who could resist such a proposal?'

'You must be out of your mind,' flashed Tammy,
suddenly spurred into retaliation, 'if you think I'd

lie here in the hope that you might return!' She attempted to sit, but he caught her wrists and pinned her arms down above her head.

'Then tell me, dear lady, what you're doing here?' His eyes glinted with malicious humour, as intent on degrading her as she was on escaping.

Completely restricted in her movements Tammy said furiously, 'You wouldn't understand.'

'Try me,' he suggested lightly.

'Like hell I will!' she returned.

'Tut, tut,' he reproved, 'that's twice you've used that word. Most unladylike.'

'But I'm not a lady, am I?' she cried passionately. 'I'm a charwoman, or whatever term you like to use, and I hate you, and I demand that you let me go!'

His face firmed, eyes granite-like as he looked down on her in cold disapproval. He swore violently beneath his breath and then, surprisingly, he got up from the bed. Opening a drawer, he took out a handkerchief and without another word left the room.

Tammy scrambled to her feet, bewildered by his unexpected action but relieved that he had not forced a confession from her—sure, though, that it would only be a matter of hours before he recovered her passport and threw her off the ship.

She did not see him again that day and could not stem the feeling of apprehension, hoping that Emil would not cause trouble. If he refused to give up her belongings, what then? Would Hugo start a fight and demand that he hand them over, or would he perhaps call in the police and let them deal with it?

It was late evening before he returned, and by this

time Tammy had worked herself up into quite a state. She had hoped that he would come straight and tell her the results of his discussions, but instead he joined his friends and although she hovered in the background he completely disregarded her.

When everyone had retired, and Tammy herself had gone to bed, she knew she would not sleep until she found out what had happened. Belting a short cotton dressing gown round her waist and pushing her toes into slippers, she made her way upstairs to the corridor where the main staterooms were.

Keeping her fingers crossed that she would meet no one, she crept along the carpeted floor until she reached Hugo's room at the end. She tapped on the door, reluctant to make too much noise in case any of the others came out to see who it was disturbing him at such a late hour.

When there was no answer she was compelled to knock harder, biting her lip anxiously. Everywhere was so quiet that she jumped violently when the door suddenly swung open. Hugo, wearing only a black and gold silk dressing gown, frowned when he saw who his visitor was.

'What do you want?' he asked thickly, running his fingers through tousled hair and peering at her as if he was only half awake and could not believe what he saw.

'A word with you,' she whispered. 'Can I come in, before anyone sees us here like this?'

A slow smile curved his lips, but still he blocked the doorway. 'Their reactions could prove interesting, especially Andrea's. Do you know she's already jealous of you? Stupid, isn't it, when neither of us can stand the sight of the other?'

Oh, God, if he only knew! Tammy went quite cold inside and although the night was relatively warm she began to shiver violently.

Hugo dragged her inside muttering something about the stupidity of women walking about in the middle of the night with next to nothing on.

'If you'd had the good manners to come and tell me what happened today,' she returned hotly, not afraid to shout now that the door was shut, 'I wouldn't have had to seek you out. You might have known I wouldn't be able to sleep wondering whether you'd got my passport back.'

'What makes you so sure I went to see Conin?' he asked abruptly.

'You told me yesterday in no uncertain terms that you couldn't wait to get me off your ship.'

'And you on your part are equally anxious to leave?'

He paused, seeming to wait for an answer, and Tammy shrugged. 'It's not much fun being kept prisoner and spending all my days slaving to keep your rotten boat clean.'

His brows rose fractionally. 'I'm sorry if I'm such a hard taskmaster. Miss Harriet never complained, she seemed to cope adequately.'

'But she's gone down sick,' returned Tammy, 'and don't try to tell me that it wasn't overwork that caused it, because I shan't believe you.'

'Please yourself,' he returned acidly, 'but I prefer to think that you find the work hard because you've never been used to it.'

This was perfectly true. Her small flat in London would fit into one quarter of this boat, less even, and took but a few minutes to keep tidy each day.

But she wasn't going to admit this to Hugo. 'It's no use talking to you,' she said crossly, 'you never see anyone's point of view except your own.'

Hugo studied her insolently, from the top of her reddish-brown hair, across the flimsy material which enhanced rather than hid her enticing curves, down the long length of her bare legs, to the tiny toes snuggled into satin mules.

'It never ceases to amaze me what a fireball you are for one so small.'

'And it never ceases to amaze me how inconsiderate you are, for all your airs and graces,' she fired back heatedly. 'If you treat the rest of your employees so badly I'm surprised they stay with you!'

'I can honestly say,' he said after a moment's hesitation, 'that no one has ever complained. I'm always considered a very fair boss.'

'Then all I can say,' shot back Tammy, 'is that they're either all incredibly stupid or you treat me differently.'

'If I do,' he said calmly, 'it's only because you ask for whatever you get. The others know their place and don't abuse it, but you seem to think you're different from the others and have the right to defy me.'

Tammy tilted her chin furiously. 'I don't look upon you as God, if that's what you think. To me all people are equal regardless of their financial position. Money doesn't give a person a right to dictate to someone else.'

'It does if he's paying them for their services.' Hugo's eyes were coldly angry now. 'And in that respect you're no different. I am paying you a fair wage for a fair day's work. Are you trying to tell me that you're not satisfied with the sum of money I offered?'

Tammy had never noticed before how cruel his eyes could be. She felt an actual physical pain now as they pierced through her like twin shafts of steel. She saw the unrelenting tautness of his chin and suddenly she felt afraid.

'I'm not interested in your money,' she returned tightly, 'only as a means of getting me home should I have the misfortune not to recover my own. If you'll tell me how you got on today I'll go. I can see you don't like having your sleep disturbed.'

'Especially by a fiery little redhead like you,' he thrust back.

Tammy checked a hasty retort, realising he had said this deliberately knowing how much she hated her hair being referred to in that manner.

'As a matter of fact,' he said slowly, 'I didn't see Conin. He was out of town.'

Tammy could have cried. 'Why didn't you say so earlier?' she fumed, her green eyes flashing angrily. 'It would have saved me coming here, and us argu-ing—and everything.'

When Hugo suddenly smiled she could have hit him, and when he said, 'I don't know, I'm quite en-joying our little discussion,' she swung round an-grily and opened the door.

'Well, I'm not, Mr Kane,' she yelled, 'and I hope I've sufficiently disturbed your sleep so that you have trouble dropping off again!' With that she yanked the door shut with a loud bang and ran along the corridor, furiously angry with both her-self and Hugo Kane.

She had almost reached her own room when

Eddie's door opened. He wore blue striped pyjamas and yawned and stretched. 'Wazzamatter?' he blinked. 'What's all the noise about?'

'It's me,' whispered Tammy loudly, 'I was having a row with Hugo. I guess the whole ship heard, but I don't care, not any longer. I don't give a damn about your employer, do you hear? He's the most impossible, inconsiderate, insufferable person I've ever met!'

Eddie was motioning her to keep quiet, but Tammy was past caring. 'He treats me like a galley slave, shouts at me like a child, insults me by calling my hair red, and then expects me to respect him. Have you ever heard the like? Honestly, Eddie, I think I shall go mad! Have you got any whisky in there, I have a fancy to drown my sorrows?'

'I wouldn't advise you to go inside that cabin, Miss Swift.'

Tammy swung round, realising now why Eddie had been gesticulating so frantically.

'Not if you don't want a repetition of the other night. Marchant's not to be trusted, you should know that by now.'

'So who can I talk to on this damn boat?' she cried, glaring defiantly up into the hard rock-like face. 'I'm going slowly insane, do you know that? If I don't get off soon I shall be a raving lunatic!'

'Don't exaggerate,' Hugo said sharply, 'and you, Marchant, get back inside, I'll deal with Tammy.'

His grip on her arm was like a vice. It would have been futile to struggle. She managed a weak smile at Eddie as she was dragged into her cabin, and if she hadn't been so livid she would have laughed at the bewildered expression on his face.

He had plainly never seen Hugo in such a mood before, or else he was wondering what had gone on between them that could have caused such violent clashes of temperament.

Inside Tammy stood rebelliously silent, her arms folded in front of her, her eyes staring in defiance. At length she said, 'Why did you follow me, Mr Kane?'

'Because I don't like my door being banged, waking up the whole bloody ship.'

'It's your own fault.' Tammy tilted her chin higher. 'You should know what to expect when you make me angry.'

'When *I* make you angry?' he scoffed. 'I've never seen you anything else. I'm beginning to see why your fiancé called the wedding off.'

'David and I never argued,' she defended hotly, 'at least not until he declared his intention of flying to New Zealand.'

'And now it's all over, is it? I haven't seen you hurrying to wire him, to let him know you're perfectly safe.'

In answer Tammy fetched her jacket from the wardrobe and pulled out of its pocket the letter she had penned a few days ago. 'As a matter of fact I have written,' she said drily. 'But trying to post it was another thing. Perhaps you'd like to oblige?'

Hugo plucked the envelope from her fingers, studied the name and address, and then with slow deliberation tore it into pieces which he let flutter to the floor.

'Why have you done that?' demanded Tammy wildly, angrily.

'Because, for one thing, I don't think you really

love him, and another, I don't want him hotfooting
it over here accusing me of taking away his girl.'

'That's a laugh,' she cried. 'I wouldn't be interested in you if you were the last man on earth!'
The lie caught in her throat and she turned the sob
into a cough, hoping he would not notice.

'*I* know that,' he agreed coolly, 'but would he? It
could look mighty suspicious, and I have enough to
contend with Emil Conin at the moment without
an irate lover breathing down my neck.'

'He'll find out one day,' she said tiredly, wishing
he would leave and let her go to bed.

Hugo nodded. 'But when he does things will
probably have sorted themselves out, and he'll thank
me for saving you from the wicked Emil Conins of
this world.'

How about the wicked Hugo Kanes, she wanted
to cry out, who break a girl's heart without knowing it, and treat her abominably? If he didn't go
soon, she decided, she would break down and cry,
and what would he think of her then?

'Have you nothing more to say for yourself?' he
goaded. 'Don't tell me little Tammy Swift is lost for
words.'

'I'm tired,' she said quietly, adding to herself, 'and
heartbroken, and disappointed.' It was becoming
clearer with every passing minute that Hugo Kane
did not like her, but, being the man he was, having
committed himself, he would see this thing through.

'In that case,' he said, 'I'll go. Though I doubt
your conscience will let you sleep after waking the
whole ship.'

Had she really done that? thought Tammy, horrified. Had everyone heard their argument? Would

her name be a constant source of conjecture to-morrow? 'You're exaggerating,' she rallied, more to convince herself than him. 'I wasn't shouting that loud.'

'But you did bang my door and I did see several heads popping out to see what all the commotion was about.'

'And you let them see you running after me, like that?' queried Tammy, staring at his hard-muscled tanned legs protruding from beneath his dressing-gown, the expanse of powerful chest where it gaped open above the belt.

'You came to me in a not much better state of dress,' he returned lightly.

'But I was careful to let no one see me.'

'Except Eddie. Dear Eddie, always ready with a shoulder to cry on. You certainly pick them, don't you, Tammy?'

'Oh, get out!' she cried miserably. 'I've had enough tonight, can't you see that? I can't take any more!'

He looked at her for a long time. Finally he nodded, 'You do look all in,' and to her surprise pressed a kiss to her forehead. 'Goodnight, Tammy. Don't forget, bright and early in the morning. No one likes being kept waiting for their breakfast when there's another brilliant Mediterranean day waiting for them outside.'

Quietly he let himself out and Tammy climbed wearily back into bed. His reference to the weather made her envy the guests their relaxed, peaceful life. All they did each day was soak up the sun, play deck quoits, swim or ski, or shop in the expensive but beautiful town. Everything was laid on for their pleasure. Not for them an early start. They could get up what time they liked, whereas she had to be up early—in case they were. When they ate, she worked. When they relaxed, she worked.

All of a sudden it felt too much for her and she broke down into a deluge of tears. This should have been her honeymoon, not a drudge. Still crying, Tammy slept, tossing fitfully all night through and waking instantly when the alarm rang.

Her reflection in the mirror was haggard and she piled on the make-up in an effort to disguise the shadows beneath her eyes and the pallor of her skin.

Chips, as ever sympathetic, passed her a cup of strong, steaming coffee. He said nothing: he did not need to. He must know what had happened, the whole ship would know, but she must hold her head up high and not let any of it get her down.

Eddie came into the kitchen next. 'Morning, Tam,' he said gently. 'Everything okay?'

She nodded and carried on drinking her coffee, grateful that he was not pursuing the matter.

When Karina came in she looked at the company expectantly. 'Anyone know what was happening last night? I heard the most frightful bang and lots of explosive conversation, but I was too tired to drag myself out of bed and have a look.'

Tammy looked at Eddie.

He looked at her and then towards Karina. 'I heard nothing, did you, Chips? You must have been dreaming, Karina. I'd forget it, if I was you.'

'But I'm sure I heard something,' persisted the plump hairdresser. 'How about you, Tammy?'

Tammy could stand no more. She got up and left.

If they wanted to talk they could, so long as she wasn't there to hear it.

She laid the table and then went up on to the deck. Luckily it was deserted and none of the other ships in the harbour showed signs of life. Sinking down on to one of the cushioned seats, she dropped her head back and closed her eyes. Soon she was asleep.

The next thing Tammy knew her shoulder was being vigorously shaken. She lifted heavy eyelids and through a blur saw the impeccable Andrea. 'Is this what Hugo pays you for?' she asked in that proud little voice of hers. 'I shouldn't like to be in your shoes when he finds out.'

Fully awake now, Tammy said, 'He won't, unless you tell him.'

'And I shall, make no bones about that,' hissed the dark girl sharply, 'and don't think I didn't hear you in his room last night. We all heard you, shouting and bawling like some shameless hussy! As far as I'm concerned the sooner you're off this ship the better!'

'That goes for me too,' returned Tammy, and had the satisfaction of seeing Andrea look slightly taken aback.

'What I can't understand is why he came after you,' continued the other girl, and there was a slight softening of her tone as she realised full well that she would not get the answer to this question if she persisted in harassing Tammy.

Even so Tammy stared at her coldly. 'And you never will, not from me. Why don't you try asking Hugo?'

'Oh, I will, never fear.'

But somehow Tammy didn't think she would. Andrea was frightened now that Hugo was showing an interest in Tammy, and to show her jealousy would get her nowhere. In fact it would frighten him off, Tammy knew that. She knew more about Hugo than Andrea was aware.

CHAPTER EIGHT

HUGO disappeared again after breakfast, but whether he was attempting to find Emil Tammy did not know, and she certainly didn't intend asking him, not after last night. He would tell her in his own good time once he had seen this elusive man. Perhaps Conin would not prove too awkward and refuse Hugo her possessions.

For the rest of that day Tammy attempted to keep out of the way of the guests—not, she told herself, because it bothered her what they said, but the truth of the matter was, it did. Despite her quick temper and ability to stand up for herself Tammy was a sensitive girl, and the thought that she might be the object of unkind gossip disturbed her.

The Murrays would not say anything malicious, she knew that, but the Andersons, and Andrea, would certainly have a ball speculating on what had happened.

She could not avoid them all day, though. Mealtimes, for instance, when she was compelled to wait at the table, Tammy had to pretend not to see their knowing looks and cool asides. Maggie alone smiled kindly and Tammy held on to that, clamping a smile to her own lips and making believe that there was nothing amiss.

Tammy was surprised when Hugo had not returned in time for the evening meal, and felt disturbed when he had still not put in an appearance before she went to bed.

Suppose he had got involved in a fight? Suppose he was hurt? She went cold at the thought. There was a thousand and one things that could have happened—and it was all her fault. Eventually she fell asleep, waking in the early hours still not knowing whether he had returned or not.

She didn't dare go along to his room, not after what had happened yesterday. He must be back, she had to content herself, and managed to fall asleep again.

Sure enough, at breakfast Hugo was there, but apart from a courteous, 'Good morning, Tammy,' when he saw her, that was all. Not a word about yesterday, nothing about his meeting with Emil Conin, that was supposing he had seen him. She could only assume he had; for all she knew he could have been away on some other business not concerning her at all.

The day dragged, all the time Tammy expecting Hugo to seek her out. But he didn't. In fact Andrea was never out of his company; they laughed and joked, kissed and cuddled, until Tammy felt ill with it all and shut herself in her room.

Hugo didn't love Andrea, so why pretend he did? It would be all the harder for her when he finally made the break. He was being unnecessarily cruel.

But then he was a cruel man; she had found that out herself.

Several days went by and still Hugo made no direct contact with her. He was civil enough, in front of the others, but he never sought her out when she was alone, and Tammy was too proud now to approach him herself.

It was hard, not knowing what was going on, or how much longer she was compelled to remain on board the *Flying Queen*, but there was little she could do under the circumstances.

Eddie, too, seemed to be keeping out of her way and she guessed he respected Hugo too much to risk angering him again. She knew how much his job meant to him and in a way rather admired his self-discipline. Girls to Eddie were the next best thing to working on this ship and for him to deny himself the pleasure of female company must be very hard indeed.

But that did not help her, it only added to her loneliness. Admittedly there was Karina, but often the woman was busy, or else the salon was closed. Chips too always seemed to be doing something or other and although he was ready to lend a sympathetic ear, part of his mind was concentrating on the task in hand, and consequently Tammy did not get much consolation from that quarter.

It was on the Friday night when she was clearing the table after dinner that Hugo said to her, 'Oh, Tammy, I'd like to see you in my room afterwards.'

'Very well,' she said, but she did not rush, taking her time over her own meal and staying to talk to Karina before she eventually made her way to his cabin.

His door was ajar and she let herself in, closing it quietly behind her. At first she thought he had not heard. He was staring at a picture on the wall opposite, a modern painting of the Palace in Monaco, which stood on the rock up above the harbour where they were now anchored. With its crenellated fish-tail towers and handsome arcaded courtyard it presented an impressive scene.

'So you've come at last.' Hugo turned and switched his attention to Tammy. 'I'd begun to think you were going to ignore my request.'

'I almost did,' she said, stung into a heated reply. 'You've ignored me for the past week, so why should I come running when you call?'

'No reason, no reason at all,' he said calmly, much to her annoyance. 'Would you care for a drink?' Without waiting for an answer he crossed the room and pressed a button on the wall. Even though Tammy had cleaned this room many times she had not known of the existence of a drinks cupboard and was amazed to see the panel swing open.

He handed her a dry sherry and indicated that she should sit on one of the ornate gilded chairs. She perched on the edge, sipped her drink, and looked up at him enquiringly.

'What do you want me for?' she asked bluntly.

'Does there have to be a reason?' he parried mildly. 'Couldn't it be that I want your company? As you rightly pointed out, we haven't seen much of each other lately.'

'And whose fault is that?' she scoffed. 'Here's me, been half out of my mind wondering how much longer I've got to stay in this dreary place and you calmly say you want my *company*! I thought you might have some news for me, that's why I came. If you haven't—well, I'll go right now.'

She got up, but he pushed her back down again, not too gently. 'Don't be silly.'

'Silly?' she almost screamed. 'You seem to be playing some sort of game, Mr Kane! I don't know what motive you have for keeping me here, but whatever it is I think it stinks. I want my passport back, and if you won't get it then I'll go to the police, or the British Consul, or whoever it is I have to see.'

All the bottled-up emotion Tammy had felt this last week came to the surface. She was furious, and Hugo knew it, and for some reason it amused him.

'Ready for battle, Red?'

'With you—any time,' she slung back, and finished her drink in one swallow, holding out the glass with a rigid arm. 'I'll have another, *if you don't mind.*'

He obliged, smiling to himself all the time, enraging her further.

'Thank you,' she said with exaggerated politeness, sitting back on the uncomfortable chair and crossing one leg neatly over the other. 'What shall we drink to, the safe return of my papers?'

'You could try that,' he agreed amiably, leaning back against the wall at her side and allowing his amused eyes to rest on her tense face.

'But it wouldn't help?' she queried. 'Is that what you're insinuating? If you ask me I don't think you're trying at all.'

'What makes you think that?' His eyes widened innocently.

He was so handsome, damn him, she thought furiously, and she loved him so desperately that it was going to be difficult to keep up this aggression. It was easy when he was angry too, but in this lighthearted mood she knew it would not be long before she succumbed and joined him in laughing at herself. 'Because if you were you would have contacted Emil Conin by now,' she stormed.

'Perhaps I have.'

'I would have known,' she returned confidently. 'You would have told me. What I want to know is why you haven't. Is it because, despite what you told me about the number of people wanting jobs on these boats, you have difficulty in finding someone to replace me?'

'Someone as attractive,' he agreed, 'or someone with whom I would enjoy sparring. I've never met a girl quite like you before. I find you stimulating company, Tammy, do you know that?'

'Big deal,' she said disrespectfully. 'You stimulate me as well. I feel I could kill you sometimes!'

He nodded approvingly. 'A good, healthy reaction. I wouldn't have you any other way.'

She sipped her drink and stared at him rebelliously. 'So what happens next? Do we sit here all night arguing, just so that it will please my lord and master, or do we call it a truce and make civilised conversation—or better still, shall I leave and return to the haven of my own cabin?'

'You've spent enough time there recently,' he said, surprising her that he had kept tabs on her whereabouts. 'In fact, I had the distinct impression that you were avoiding me.'

Or you me, she thought tightly, but she said, 'Oh, really, now why would I want to do that, *Mr* Kane?'

His lips firmed, but he managed to smile as he replied, 'After our little—er—fiasco, the other night. I mean, my guests did get the wrong impression, or hadn't you heard? They think there's something going on between you and me. I've had the devil of a job persuading Andrea that we're sworn enemies.'

So that accounted for the fuss he had paid Andrea recently, nevertheless it did not please her to think that there was a rumour going about the ship that she was having an affair with Hugo. She had deliberately shut her ears to all gossip, perhaps afraid that something like this might happen. Now she felt both humiliated and angry.

'Perhaps we ought to make a public announcement,' she said primly.

'That we're having an affair?' he said, deliberately misunderstanding her. 'Are we? I didn't know, but I'm willing if you are.'

'You know what I mean,' she cried tensely.

'It would be very pleasant,' he continued, as though she had not spoken. 'Yes, a most pleasing experience.'

Tammy stood up and turned her back on him. 'I don't know how you can joke about such a thing! I don't find it funny.'

'Nor do I,' he assured her. 'I was quite serious.'

She shot him a startled look. 'I'm not that type of girl.'

'No?' His brows rose questioningly. 'You didn't seem averse to Marchant making a fuss of you. If I hadn't come in when I did who knows what might have happened.'

Tammy guessed there was no point in denying that she had not encouraged Eddie; he wouldn't believe her, not in his present mood. He would assume she was making excuses. She shrugged, 'Think what you like,' and turned away again.

'We're going to Corsica tomorrow,' he said suddenly, 'for a couple of days.'

Tammy felt sure he was doing this deliberately to prolong the time of her departure. 'I think you're scared of Emil Conin,' she said contemptuously, 'otherwise you'd have seen him before now and I could be gone.'

'What's the matter, don't you like the idea? I thought you would enjoy the opportunity of visiting another country.'

'In the right company I might,' she said disrespectfully. 'But with you life's one sheer round of hell.'

She was not looking at him as she spoke, but she sensed his sudden tenseness. Even so she was not prepared when his hand dropped on her shoulder, twisting her round so that she was compelled to look into his hard, dark eyes.

'I mean it,' she cried defiantly, without giving him the opportunity to speak. 'You must know I'm not enjoying the situation, that I find the work a drudge and the company totally unacceptable.'

'By that I presume you're referring to me,' he said harshly. 'You ask for all you get, Tammy. I'm quite prepared to call a truce, but each time we meet you treat me to a dose of that red-hot temper of yours.'

'Only because you goad me.'

He shook her impatiently. '*I* goad *you*? My God, Tammy, you want to take a good long look at yourself.'

She felt herself go limp in his arms. 'Can I go

now?' Loving him so desperately how could she possibly respond when he treated her like this? She almost felt she hated him.

'Had enough?' he sneered, making no attempt to lift his hands. 'I've won, have I, Tammy? You no longer want to fight. Pity, I never thought you'd give in so easily.'

'I don't know what you're talking about,' she cried hotly. 'All I know is that I'm sick and tired of your insults and I want to go to my cabin. If we're going to Corsica tomorrow I suppose I shall have to be up early, so I'd better try and get some sleep. I doubt whether I shall, though, now you've succeeded in unsettling me yet again.'

His hands slid from her shoulders to the small of her back and he pulled her against him. Tammy's first instinct was to struggle, but she felt tired, far too tired to find the energy to resist, so she allowed herself to be held against his warm, hard body.

When he spoke he sounded disappointed, as if he had expected her to object. 'What's up, Tammy, given up altogether? If you can't beat 'em, join 'em, is that it?' He let her go. 'Run along,' he said, as if talking to a child, 'get your beauty sleep. As you rightly assume, I shall expect you up at six.'

He turned away as he spoke and she had no way of telling his reaction to her passiveness. She herself was disappointed. For once she had looked forward to his caress, had felt the need for physical contact and the comfort it would give her. She gazed at his broad back for a few moments before pivoting swiftly and leaving the room.

She somehow had the impression that he was as disappointed as she, which was stupid, for how could he be when she meant so little to him?

Back in her cabin Tammy got ready for bed, and despite her assertion to the contrary she was looking forward to Corsica. A change of scenery might do her good, pull her out of the lethargy she was beginning to feel.

Surprisingly she slept, waking at five-thirty feeling completely refreshed and amazingly cheerful. Soon they were on their way and although she would have loved to watch as they moved out of the harbour she knew that she must carry on with her work if she did not want to incur Hugo's wrath yet again.

Anyone would think I was frightened of him, she thought, and assured herself that it was a sense of duty, no more, that made her so conscientious.

Corsica, decided Tammy, was beautiful. They were approaching the island, and borne out to them on a warm land breeze was the scent of the maquis. 'Which,' Eddie told her, as he stood by her side at the rail, 'is scrubland which covers vast areas of the island.'

Beyond the buildings which circled the shores of Ajaccio rose Alpine-like peaks, the dark purple of distant forests and the shine of olive groves, which rippled like silver threads beaneath the breath of the wind.

Two hours later they had dropped both anchors and were all eager to go ashore and explore. To Tammy's surprise Hugo had come up to her and said, 'Go ahead, enjoy yourself. No more meals on board today, your time is your own.'

Eddie at her elbow, overhearing, had immediately

taken her arm and led her away, shrugging almost offensively when Hugo had said, 'Watch it, Marchant, any funny business and you'll have me to contend with.'

As soon as they had set foot on the island Eddie hired a car and told Tammy that he was going to show her some of Corsica's delights. She would have preferred today to explore Ajaccio and perhaps gone sightseeing tomorrow, but it seemed rude to reject his offer and she had climbed somewhat reluctantly into the old black car, hoping it was more reliable that it looked.

Once out of the town their route took them up into the mountains, through dark, brooding forests of chestnut trees, beside gently sloping vineyards, and through villages where the locals sat out in the shade of the narrow streets playing cards or simply talking. It gave them breathtaking views of golden beaches, of flocks of sheep in fields. The contrasting scenery quite took Tammy's breath away and she scarcely spoke, spending the whole time looking out of the window.

At closer quarters she realised that the maquis varied in height from a few inches to several feet and consisted of myrtle, heather, broom, wild lavender, rosemary, and several other plants which she could not identify.

Occasionally thickets of ilex and cork oak broke up the dense purple vegetation, making her realise how easy it used to be for bandits to hide. She had heard the expression, 'Taking to the maquis.' Now she knew what it meant.

They travelled slowly, stopping once for food but mainly riding around. There was very little traffic on the roads besides themselves and when, in one of the unpopulated areas of the island, the car gave a sudden, deep-throated roar and jerked and jolted to a grinding halt, Tammy realised instantly that they could be stuck for hours before help came—unless Eddie could sort out their trouble.

They looked at each other helplessly.

'What's wrong?' she asked.

'Don't ask me,' he said expressively, opening his door. He lifted the bonnet and spent the next few minutes tinkering around.

Tammy got out and watched him, perceiving unhappily as the seconds ticked by that he had no idea what he was doing. He might be a first class steward, but car mechanics were completely beyond him.

'I'm sorry,' he said at length. 'I can't quite put my finger on it.'

'So what are we going to do?' asked Tammy, looking about her and shuddering. The maquis which had earlier looked so romantic now seemed full of danger. Who knew who might be lurking in that dense undergrowth? Perhaps waiting to attack, to rob them? Her imagination ran riot.

She shuddered and Eddie put his arm across her shoulders. 'Don't worry, Tammy. Someone will come before long and if they can't help us at least they can fetch someone who can.'

'I'd rather walk than remain here,' she said plaintively. 'You know as well as I do that we haven't seen a car in the last hour. We could be here all night. How far is the next village?'

'I don't know,' admitted Eddie, shamefaced. 'I think this road leads back to Ajaccio, but I'm not certain. I do know, though, that it won't be long before we're rescued.' He grinned. 'Keep your chin up, Tam, you're perfectly safe with me.'

She was not so sure. Eddie was all right for a laugh, a bit of fun, but in an emergency? Suddenly she wanted Hugo. He would know what to do. He would be able to mend the car. Her faith in him surprised her and she looked at Eddie, her green eyes wide and shadowed. 'What will Hugo say?'

He snorted derisively. 'A time like this and you think of him? To hell with what Hugo says! He can't blame me this time, not when the stupid car won't go,' and he kicked the wheel viciously.

His anger released Tammy's and she said hotly, 'If you were half the man he is you'd know what to do. Stay here if you like, but I'm going to walk.'

Eddie looked hurt. 'So there really is something going between you two?' and when Tammy did not answer, he added cuttingly, 'How about your boyfriend, where does he fit into the picture? You were so eager to assure me of your love for him, yet all the time it's Hugo you fancy. I never thought you were like that, Tammy, I really didn't.'

'So now you know,' she cried defensively, 'and I certainly wish he was here now. He'd be able to get the car going, that much I know.'

'Proper little champion, aren't you?' he sneered. 'I wonder if he knows how fortunate he is?'

'Don't you dare tell him!' Tammy all at once realised the enormity of her confession, and unable to stand arguing with Eddie any longer she walked on in the direction they had been travelling.

She wanted to look over her shoulder to see whether he followed, hoping he would, even though at this moment she did not particularly like him.

But to turn would admit that she was scared, and a condescending Eddie would be worse than an argumentative one.

A superb sunset which had coloured the sky crimson now turned into instant darkness and Tammy walked for a quarter of an hour before she saw a flicker of light in the distance. Almost crying with relief, she started to run, stumbling in her haste and sprawling full length on the floor, grazing her knees and hands.

The vehicle that approached was a lorry of sorts, but even before it reached her Tammy could hear loud, vulgar singing in rough Corsican voices, and the vehicle swerved from side to side across the road. She shrank back into the brushwood, preferring to walk all the way back to Ajaccio rather than face what to her appeared to be a band of drunken peasants.

Another hour passed and still no sign of habitation. Tears ran freely down her cheeks and she wished with all her heart that Hugo would appear. She could stand his chastisement, bear the wrath of his tongue, if he would only take her back to the boat.

When a vehicle approached from behind she shrank back again into the roadside, appreciating that it might be help but afraid it might yet again be someone who would do her more harm than good.

As soon as it went by she realised it was Eddie. By some miracle he had got the car going! She ran out into the road and raced after him, calling his name at the top of her voice, wishing it was light so that he could see her.

Just as she had thought he had not heard, the car braked violently and he came running back towards her. 'Oh, Eddie,' she cried, falling into his arms, forgetting her earlier antipathy. 'Oh, Eddie, I was so frightened!'

He led her back to the car, saying grimly, once she was seated, 'It would have served you right if you'd got accosted. It was a stupid thing to do, running away like that. I knew help would arrive sooner or later.'

'How could you?' she demanded savagely. 'And if it was that load of drunken peasants who helped you then I'm glad I wasn't there.'

'I asked them if they'd seen you,' he said. 'I was worried when they said they hadn't.'

'I'd have been worried if they had,' continued Tammy angrily. 'Can you imagine what they'd have done to me?'

'You're letting your imagination get the better of you,' he said quietly, but she knew that he was thinking the same.

Neither of them spoke after that and when they eventually arrived back at the boat they crept quietly on board, both of the same mind that with good fortune they might not have been missed.

Their luck was in, the *Flying Queen* was empty. Eddie's strained face relaxed and even Tammy was conscious of a feeling of relief.

'I don't know about you,' she said, 'but I'm going straight to bed. I've had enough for one day.'

She ran a bath and lay soaking in the perfumed water, still unable to believe that Hugo had not discovered them missing. No doubt he and the others had gone into the town for the night and had not really expected her and Eddie back until late.

Her hands and knees were sore and she smoothed in some antiseptic cream, leisurely brushing her hair before stepping back into her cabin. She felt tired and was smothering a yawn when the sight of Hugo sitting on the edge of her bed drove all thoughts of sleep from her mind.

'Where the devil have you been?' he asked harshly, rising to his feet and crossing towards her. His face was tight, his lips grim, and his eyes cruelly piercing.

Before she could answer his hands shot out and gripped her arms so fiercely that within seconds she could feel them tingling. He shook her angrily and violently and her head flopped on her shoulders, her teeth chattering.

'What have you and Marchant been up to?' he demanded. 'Tell me, Tammy, tell me, before I wring your bloody neck!'

CHAPTER NINE

TAMMY thought Hugo would never stop shaking her, and already weakened through tiredness and lack of food, she slumped against him. When he flung her away in disgust she fell limply back across the bed.

It was then that he saw her knees, bleeding now through contact with the rough material of his suit. 'Has Marchant molested you?' he blazed. 'If he has, Tammy, by God I'll——'

'No!' she cried, shaking her head drunkenly. It felt so heavy on her shoulders, almost as though it didn't belong there. 'No! We broke down—I was walking—and I fell, that's all. Eddie had nothing to do with it.'

He stared at her disbelievingly for a full minute. 'Why didn't he save you?'

'He—he wasn't there. I was—alone.' Her wide emerald eyes seemed to fill her whole face.

'Why?' The question was like a gunshot, right there in the room. 'Don't answer, I'll find out for myself.'

When he disappeared she knew he had gone to Eddie. His cabin was two doors away from her own, but even so she could hear their raised voices and cringed inwardly.

It was not all Eddie's fault. She was the one who had insisted on walking, she could have stayed with him. And he could have come with you, argued an inner voice. But somehow she knew she must try to defend him.

Pulling on her housecoat, she stumbled out of her cabin and into Eddie's. His door was wide open, but she closed it behind her.

'Keep out of this,' grated Hugo, glancing at her briefly as she thrust her way into the room. 'This is between Marchant and me.'

He had his hand round the chief steward's throat and Eddie was looking like a frightened rabbit. There was no fight in him and Tammy wondered why she bothered. He was nothing but a weakling and a coward.

'You can't blame Eddie,' she cried passionately, still feeling the need to defend. 'He didn't want me to walk.'

'Shut up!' Hugo did not even spare her a glance. 'Get back to your cabin. I'll deal with you later.'

But Tammy found the strength seeping back into her limbs and she flung herself at him, trying to drag his hands away from Eddie's throat. 'Leave him alone, it wasn't his fault! We argued and I ran away, it's as simple as that.'

With one powerful thrust Hugo sent her spinning across the room, but he let Eddie go and the younger man cowered back against the wall.

'I—I'm sorry, Hugo, really I am. As Tammy said, we had this row—I knew she'd come to no harm. I wouldn't have let her go otherwise.'

'You'd broken down yet you found time to argue?' demanded Hugo. 'I find that hard to believe. What were you arguing about, who should go for help?'

Tammy, watching Eddie, saw a light come into his eyes, as if he had suddenly thought of a way of saving himself. 'As a matter of fact it was you we were discussing,' he said smoothly. 'Tammy said——'

'Don't you dare!' Tammy shot across the room, her cheeks flaming. 'Eddie, I'll never forgive you if you——'

But as she had known, Hugo's curiosity was now aroused and he said loudly, 'Go on, Marchant, what did Tammy say?'

'That I was only half the man you are.'

Whatever Tammy had expected it had not been this, not something against himself. She was too shocked to do anything more than look at him open-mouthed.

'I mean,' he continued plaintively, 'how would you like it if someone said that to you about another man? I'm afraid I accused her of carrying a torch for you and it was then that she walked away.'

He waited for Hugo to speak, and when he didn't, when he merely looked at Eddie, a slow smile creeping over his face, the younger man continued in an ingratiating voice that sickened Tammy, 'You can't blame me for not following her, can you, Hugo, not after that?'

If he had not tacked on those last few words Tammy felt he might have got away with it, but Hugo's face now hardened again and he said forcefully, 'You're a coward, Marchant. Didn't you think fit to warn her that there might be bandits lurking in the maquis, men on the run ready to commit murder without any provocation?'

Tammy left the cabin; she had seen enough to turn her off Eddie for ever.

She was in bed when Hugo again opened the door and came into her room. She had known he would come, but it had not stopped her from getting into bed. She turned her face away tiredly. 'Go away, I have nothing more to say to you tonight.'

She did not hear his footsteps across the room, but she felt his weight upon the edge of the bed causing her to roll very slightly towards him. Her fingers were clenched into fists beneath the sheets as she waited for him to speak.

'Tammy,' he said softly, after a few long seconds had passed when all she heard was his deep regular breathing. 'Tammy, are you really all right? Eddie told me about those men in the lorry. When I think what they could have done to you in their drunken stupor——'

'They didn't see me,' she murmured, her voice muffled in the pillow. 'I hid in the brushwood.'

'Thank God for that,' he breathed quietly.

He sounded so relieved, so genuinely concerned, that she turned her head enquiringly. 'Do you care? Wouldn't you have said that it served me right if anything had happened?'

'I'm not quite so callous as that, despite what you may think.' A wry smile flickered across his face. 'And I'm more annoyed with Marchant than you, but it doesn't mean to say I approve of your going off with him like that.'

'He wasn't to know the car would break down.' she said, surprising herself by defending Eddie.

'But he did know he was no mechanic. He should have kept to the main roads.'

'Does it matter now?' asked Tammy wearily. 'It's over and done with and I'm not likely to make the same mistake again.'

'Does that mean that your passion for my chief steward is cured?' The dark eyes studied her sardonically, an ironic smile tugging at the corners of his mouth.

Tammy refused to look at him. 'He was nothing more than a friend,' she said woodenly. 'I'm not even sure he's that any more.'

'I'm glad to hear it, but just to make sure, you can tag along with me tomorrow. I'm going to show Tom and Maggie the house where Napoleon was born, and also the Napoleonic museum.'

Tammy loved anything historical and looked up at him now, her face all at once alive with interest. 'I'd like that, but won't Andrea mind? You know how she feels about me.'

'Andrea hates old places,' he said drily. 'She and Penny are going off by themselves, sunbathing I've no doubt on one of Corsica's fine beaches.'

'You let her go off on her own but not me?' asked Tammy suspiciously.

'She can look after herself,' he smiled. 'She's been around more than you.' He pushed himself to his feet. 'Goodnight, Tammy.'

When he had gone she lay for a long time staring up at the ceiling which reflected the movement of the water gently lapping against the sides of the boat. A full clear moon cast stark shadows across the room and all at once she felt happy—surprising, considering what a traumatic day it had been.

The Maison Bonaparte in the Rue Saint Charles was a solid three-storey house built in the early seventeenth century. On the first floor was a display of Directoire furniture bought by Napoleon's mother with a grant she had received when her house was temporarily requisitioned as an officers' billet by the English in the late seventeen hundreds.

In the main bedroom was a Louis XV bed in which the Bonapartes spent their wedding night and in which most of their children were born.

It was Napoleon's own bedroom, though, that appealed to Tammy the most. It was of almost monastic simplicity with its bare white walls. In one corner, under a cupboard, was a trapdoor from which he was said to have made his escape to the Rue Notre-Dame, though exactly why he was escaping had never been accurately determined.

After visiting the house they went to the museum with its unique collection of busts and portraits of the Imperial family. Tammy was fascinated by it all, but particularly so by the Emperor Napoleon's bronze death mask. He looked sadly youthful as if death had rejuvenated him.

The chapel and library were visited next and after lunch the cathedral. It was by far the most fascinating day Tammy had spent since leaving England, seeing a new side of Hugo and realising that he was not always unfriendly and aggressive. Of course it could be that the Murrays' presence had something to do with it; he would hardly be antagonistic towards her in front of them. Even so, Tammy found herself relaxing in his presence, laughing and talking as she had never done before.

It was late afternoon before they finally finished their explorations, and even then Tammy felt that she could have spent more time examining these priceless treasures of bygone times. But when, as they walked along the palm-lined streets, Hugo slipped his arm about her waist she forgot all about Napoleon.

Her breathing quickened with a headiness that almost made her skip along beside him. She did not care what Maggie and Tom thought—she was so happy, smiling up at Hugo, not realising how enchanting she looked with the hot Mediterranean sun turning her hair into a fiery red halo, her lips parted prettily and her unusually fair skin glowing with health and vitality.

His dark eyes narrowed as she looked at him and for a second his step faltered and the arm about her waist tightened. Then abruptly he let her go and strode ahead, frowning, as though something had upset him.

Tammy wanted to ask what was the matter, but knew she would not get a satisfactory answer, so she hurried along beside him and tried to pretend that nothing had changed. But it had. In that one inexplicable second he had altered from a carefree

companion to the brooding stranger she had become
used to.

Was it her fault? she asked herself. Had she, by
virtue of the fact that she had shown her own happiness, frightened him away? Was he afraid she might
become too interested in him?

She sighed. It hurt, his withdrawal. They had
spent such an idyllic few hours, she wished it could
have lasted for ever.

Their path took them through some of the back
streets, narrow, unevenly flagged, and with great tall
houses either side. Washing, strung on lines across
the street, fluttered in the breeze. Old men, their
faces criss-crossed with lines, sat on doorsteps half
asleep, and tattered posters adorned the walls.

It turned out that Hugo knew exactly which
beach Penny and Andrea had gone to and now an-
nounced his intention of finding them.

The *plage* was filled with bodies toasting themselves under the hot sun, and Tammy privately
thought it an impossible task. Why not let them
make their own way back? she thought discon-
tentedly as she traipsed after Hugo and the Murrays,
her feet sinking into the soft golden sands, filling
her sandals until in exasperation she took them off
and walked barefoot.

She had gone only a few steps more when she saw
them, but it was not the two women who made her
stop and stare but the man talking to them.

It looked like David. But how could it be? Wasn't
he in New Zealand? The longer she watched the
more convinced she became.

Evidently he had forgotten all about her. He was
enjoying every minute of Andrea's flirtatious, pro-

vocative manner, bending over her intimately, as though she was the only girl in the world who meant anything to him. Penny was talking too, but it was the younger, dark-haired girl who held his attention.

Tammy was seeing David as she had never seen him before. Stripped to the waist, wearing only a pair of brief white shorts, he was tanned superbly. He had not had that before he left England! Even as she watched he swung Andrea up into his arms and kissed her.

It amazed Tammy. Normally conservative in both his dress and manner, the David she knew would never dream of doing such a thing. Displays of affection were kept strictly for when they were alone.

Perhaps it wasn't him? Perhaps after all she was mistaken and it was merely someone who looked like David? That had to be the answer, for there was just no way that he could be here in Corsica.

Suddenly Andrea caught sight of Hugo striding towards them. She said something to the man at her side, who moved quickly away, soon to be lost in the throngs of people.

By the time Tammy joined them Andrea and Penny were gathering up their belongings and whether Hugo had questioned her about the unknown admirer she did not know. Nothing was mentioned on their way back to the *Flying Queen*.

Probably Hugo didn't care. By his own admittance he felt nothing for Andrea and more than likely he was relieved that she was showing interest in another man.

But Tammy herself would have liked to know who the man was, even if only for her own peace of

mind, and the uncertainty niggled her for the rest
of the day.

In the morning they returned to Monte Carlo and
Tammy's round of never-ending work began again.
She had enjoyed the break, but now wished that
Hugo would hurry and seek out Emil Conin. She
desperately wanted to go back to England. Loving
Hugo as she did it was sheer torture to be in such
close proximity each and every day knowing no good
could ever come out of it.

But almost as though he regretted the friendliness
he had shown in Corsica Hugo practically ignored
Tammy, and she felt sad and disillusioned, and even
more restless. Eddie too kept out of her way, but
when she did see him Tammy never spoke, she was
too disgusted.

She noticed also that Hugo was more offhand with
Andrea, but strangely the girl did not seem to mind.
It made Tammy wonder whether the man on the
beach, whoever he was, had anything to do with it.

After breakfast on the second morning Hugo
stayed behind and cornered Tammy as she was clearing the table. 'It has occurred to me,' he said succinctly, 'that you might want to do some more shopping. If you like I'll take you into Monte Carlo this
morning. I have business there myself and can kill
two birds with one stone, so to speak.'

He did not smile as he made his suggestion, causing Tammy to think that he had not done it out of
the kindness of his heart, but because he thought it
a necessary duty. As there were one or two personal
items she needed she nodded in agreement, keeping
her face as serious as his.

'It's very kind of you—if you're sure it's no trouble?'

'Would I have asked if it was?' he asked grimly, his grey eyes hard and impersonal. 'Hurry along, I'll meet you on the sun deck in half an hour.'

The short journey into town was accomplished in total silence and Hugo dropped Tammy off with instructions that he would meet her outside the same hotel as before in one hour's time.

'Will that be long enough?' he asked icily.

Tammy nodded, wishing he would not be so coldly aggressive on one of the rare occasions when they were alone.

It did not take her long to do her shopping, less than thirty minutes in fact, and to pass the time she wandered through the streets until she came to the Casino, an ornate building with towers at the corners and great bronze angels sitting on the roof.

In front of the Casino were the formal gardens known as the Boulingrins and she sat here for a while, admiring the host of tropical trees and cacti as large as oaks.

When it was almost time for her to meet Hugo she returned to the appointed place, to find him pacing up and down impatiently, frequently glancing at his watch.

'You're late,' he accused, the moment she appeared.

'I was early,' she replied, tossing her head haughtily, her hair swinging in silken strands about her face, 'so I went for a walk. I've been admiring the Boulingrins and the Casino—it's a very impressive place.'

He nodded indifferently. 'Let's have coffee, my throat's parched.'

On the hotel terrace they sat at the same table as before and the waiter, remembering Tammy, greeted her warmly.

The contrast between the waiter's attitude and Hugo's was so marked that Tammy could not help saying, 'Have I done something to upset you, Mr Kane? Ever since we came back from Corsica you've studiously ignored me. If there is anything I'd prefer to know.'

His lips twisted sardonically. 'Being you is enough.'

She frowned. 'I don't know what you mean.'

'I don't suppose you do,' he returned tiredly.

'If you're trying to say that you hate the sight of me and want me off your ship, why don't you do something about it?' she asked, her voice pained.

'It's not that,' he said quietly, and then on a harsher note, 'Oh, damn it, Tammy, I wish I'd never set eyes on you!'

She gasped and stared at him, her wide green eyes luminous and distressed. 'You really know how to make a girl feel uncomfortable, don't you? Do you think I feel any happier knowing that I'm only here on sufferance?'

'I don't care how you feel,' he rasped, 'I just wish to God you weren't here now!'

'You have only yourself to blame,' she returned coldly, feeling her stomach tighten and a cold shiver run down her spine. How cruel he was—how unconsciously cruel!

'And your stupidity.' His eyes were blazing now and Tammy could not be sure whether his anger was directed at himself or her.

'I didn't ask you to pick me up.'

He snorted derisively. 'Unfortunately for me I have a conscience. I couldn't stand by and let you ruin yourself, though God knows I ought to have done. You've proved you're little better than the rest of the girls Emil Conin employs.'

'If you're referring to Eddie,' declared Tammy hotly, 'you know what he can do with himself!'

His face lit up maliciously. 'Pity you had to learn the hard way.'

'Don't we all?' she asked, her breathing erratic now and her pulses beating so fast she felt sure she was going to faint. It was so warm. She brushed her hair back from her brow. 'Haven't you ever made a mistake? Are you so perfect that you know exactly what you're doing and where you're going?'

'I wouldn't be where I am today if I hadn't a very good idea,' he returned calmly. 'It takes some of us longer to grow up, that's all.'

So he thought her still a child! She clamped her teeth together and refused to answer, glad when the waiter came with their drinks, uncomfortably aware that Hugo was taking a perverse delight in watching her, insolently studying her face, until she felt ready to scream.

She gulped her coffee scalding hot, burning her mouth, but conscious only of a deep desire to get out of this place and back to the *Flying Queen*. What she couldn't understand was that if Hugo was so much against her being here why didn't he do something about it? She was totally in his hands. Until he contacted Emil Conin she was his prisoner. It was as simple as that.

Setting down her empty cup, she picked up her bag, but Hugo appeared in no hurry to leave. His coffee still untouched in front of him, his eyes glinted maliciously. 'Oh, no, Tammy, you're not going to get away from me as quickly as that.'

She glared fiercely. 'Only a few moments ago you said you wished I wasn't here. What *do* you want, Mr Kane?'

He smiled mysteriously. 'I know what I want. I also know I can't have it. But while we're out I've decided we might as well make a day of it. I'll order lunch and then we'll explore the town. You haven't seen much of Monaco yet. There's the Palace and the Oceanographical Museum—you'll like that, I know—the pseudo-Romanesque Cathedral, and then, of course, the Casino—you must go there. There's a theatre and a restaurant, a night club, several bars, and of course the Gaming Rooms. The decoration itself is worth a visit—oh,' he paused, 'I forgot, you need your passport to get in there, to make sure you're over eighteen, but never mind, there are lots more things we can see.'

He paused a moment and Tammy took the opportunity to stop his sudden outburst. 'I can't understand you! One moment you want to be rid of me, the next you're asking me to spend the day with you. Why?'

'Let's say I feel sorry for you. I hurt you by my thoughtless words and I feel I ought to make up.'

Tammy looked at him suspiciously; somehow he did not sound genuine. 'Thanks for the offer,' she said slowly, 'but no, thanks. I'd prefer to go back to the boat.'

'You mean you've had enough of my company?'

'Yes,' she said emphatically. But she didn't mean it, Lord knows she didn't. She wanted to be with

Hugo every minute of every day, but she was finding out now that the more they were together the worse it hurt. Her love was growing inside her until soon it would become too big to handle. Somehow she had to put a stop to it, and spending a day with him would never do that.

'I see.' He picked up his cup and drank quickly, wiping his lips with a napkin. Without another word he stood up.

Tammy scrambled to her own feet before he could offer his assistance. She didn't want him to touch her, she didn't even want to be close to him. The pain was excruciating.

But she needn't have worried, Hugo avoided any contact with her. In fact he did not speak again and when they got into his car she shrank against the door. When they arrived at the harbour she almost fell out in her eagerness to reach the relative safety of her own cabin.

But another shock awaited her. Standing beside Andrea on the deck, and looking at her with cold accusation, was David.

CHAPTER TEN

'DAVID!' cried Tammy hesitantly, trying to smile, feeling her lips draw themselves into a grimace but unable to fire them with any enthusiasm. 'What are you doing here?' and all the while she was thinking that it really had been him in Corsica.

Casting a fleeting glance at Andrea, Tammy saw the self-satisfied smile and didn't even have to guess what the other girl had been saying. As she looked back again at David his eyes were beyond her now fixed on Hugo as he followed her on to the boat.

Before David could answer her question Hugo spoke. 'So you're the missing fiancé? Welcome aboard. I trust that you've been well looked after in my absence?'

David said, 'Hugo Kane, I presume?' but he didn't offer to shake hands. 'I'd like a few words with Tamsin in private, if you don't mind.'

Hugo nodded and smiled, but like Tammy the smile did not quite reach his eyes. 'Feel free to use my room, it's more comfortable.'

Tammy's chin shot up defiantly. 'We'll go to my cabin,' and she marched across the deck and down the stairs, leaving David to follow. Her mind was in a turmoil. There was no way now that she could marry David, yet how could she tell him without admitting her love for Hugo? If she said there was no one else, that she had had time to think things over and decided they weren't suited, would that do? It would have to, there was no other way out.

When the door closed behind them she was conscious of the smallness of her cabin, and wished perversely that she had taken Hugo up on his offer. There was no way here that she could avoid David; a few feet was all that separated them.

Even before he spoke she was aware of a tremendous feeling of claustrophobia and swung open the porthole to try and let in some air. But it was a still, warm day and it did nothing to alleviate the stuffiness.

David waited by the door and she smiled and went across to him, holding out her arms, thinking it might help lessen the shock when she told him.

But he swung away, his eyes condemning. 'What's with you and this Hugo Kane?' he asked woodenly. 'And what are you doing here, why aren't you with Simone and Pierre? I wrote to them and they said you'd gone back to England. But I couldn't contact you there either. Now I know why.'

Tammy sank back on to the edge of the bed, her legs trembling, though she did not know why. She had nothing to hide. She had done nothing wrong.

'Pierre tried to make a pass at me,' she cried heatedly. 'Well, I wasn't going to stand for that, was I?'

David frowned, as if he could not quite believe this of his friend, but he said, 'Okay, I'll accept that, but why are you here, why didn't you go back to London?'

Tammy shrugged wryly. 'I lost my papers and my luggage, and——'

'You what?' David looked at her incredulously, his thick brows beetling over puzzled angry eyes. 'Of all the incompetent, stupid, careless things to do! Tamsin, how could you?'

She had not meant to tell him about Emil Conin, but annoyed now that he should consider her totally incapable she flashed hotly, 'It was this man's fault. He offered to help me to—to find a room. You see, I intended staying on a bit longer, to see something of France while I was here, but—well, somehow, while we were talking, my things disappeared. So he offered me this job and a room. I had no money or anything, so I accepted.'

David folded his arms and leaned back against the wall. 'A likely story,' he mocked. 'I bet that Hugo Kane fellow had it all worked out, he's probably got your passport himself and is keeping you on as cheap labour—though there looks more to it than that to me.'

'Oh, it wasn't Hugo,' cried Tammy immediately, aghast that he should think such a thing. 'His name was Emil Conin. He ran a casino in Nice and he wanted me to work as a croupier—or so I thought.' She lowered her eyes—now came the uncomfortable bit.

But David was there before her. 'Don't tell me the rest, I can guess. How could you be so gullible, Tamsin?'

He had always insisted on calling her by her full name and it irritated Tammy now, and she shook her head crossly. 'I wasn't to know, was I? Anyway, that was where Hugo came in. He saw what was happening and brought me here,' adding defensively, 'he's going to get my things back for me. He reckons that Emil Conin has them, that he's done this sort of thing before.'

David snorted. 'It's taking him long enough. It's over two weeks. What's holding him up? Or perhaps I shouldn't ask. The two of you together, is my answer, it stands out like a sore thumb.'

Tammy pressed her hands on to the edge of the bed beside her, trying hard to control her temper, which was approaching white-hot heat. She wanted to settled this matter amicably, if that was possible. Somehow she doubted it. David was at his most stubborn; in fact she could never remember seeing him like this before. He had always been so calm and courteous, a real gentleman. They had never had a

cross word in all the time they had been going together—not until he had postponed the wedding.
Perhaps that had been the beginning of the end,
only she hadn't been clever enough to see it.

'There's nothing between Hugo and me,' she said
distantly. 'He's engaged to Andrea, in case she
hasn't told you.'

By the flickering of his eyes she knew the other
girl hadn't. But he didn't admit this. He said, 'And
you're engaged to me, but from what I've heard and
can see it doesn't mean a thing. Why try to deny it,
Tamsin? Let's face it, you wouldn't have stayed
here this long if you hadn't had some hankering
after the man. You don't like boats that much.'

It was strange, but she didn't, and she had only
just remembered it! 'It's small boats I don't like,'
she amended. 'You don't know that you're on a boat
here, unless you look outside. Have you seen over it,
it's absolutely super! There's this beautiful——'

'You can't sidetrack me like that,' cut in David
tightly, digging his hands into his pockets and pulling out cigarettes and matches. He shook one out
and put it between his lips, not speaking again until
he had it satisfactorily alight. 'What I want to know
is how far things have gone between you. Are you
sleeping with him?'

'Don't be crude!' cried Tammy, pushing herself
up. 'You sound more concerned about Hugo than
the fact that I nearly got myself involved in some
racket. He's helping me, can't you understand that?'

'No, I can't,' he returned. 'Why should he? Why
should he help someone he doesn't even know?'

'Because he's kind.' Tammy's voice shook. She
swallowed with difficulty and tilting her chin looked
him in the eye and said, 'You're so busy condemn-

ing me, but how about yourself? Perhaps you think I didn't see you with Andrea in Corsica. What were you doing there, may I ask, when you told me you were going to New Zealand?'

For one second David looked taken aback, but he regained his composure quickly and said, 'I'd finished my work. I was about to fly home when I had a message to stop off at Ajaccio to see another client. The day you saw me I had a few hours to kill while I was waiting for an appointment.'

'So you spent the time amusing yourself with Andrea?'

'Can you blame me?' he asked selfconsciously. 'She's a pretty girl.'

'And not averse to encouraging lonely bachelors?' returned Tammy. 'How did you find out I was here?'

For the first time he looked embarrassed. 'I—I thought I'd say goodbye to Andrea. She'd told me which boat she was on and that she was leaving the next morning. When I came to the harbour and saw you on deck I could hardly believe my eyes.'

'Why didn't you speak to me then?'

'The boat was already moving.'

'So you went back to England and then flew out again to Monte to tax me with these false accusations?'

'I don't regard them as false,' he said coldly. 'Andrea's been telling me how much time you and Kane spend together, that you actually spent one night in his cabin.'

'That's a lie!' snapped Tammy. 'I went to see him, yes, but I didn't stay all night. I wanted to ask how much longer he was going to take to recover my passport.'

'And you had to go to his room in the middle of the night to do that? Really, Tamsin, credit me with a little sense!'

Tammy tossed her head scornfully. 'I don't see why I should take this from you when you're clearly as bad. You fancy Andrea, don't you?' She snatched off her engagement ring and held it in front of his eyes. 'Here, you're free. Go to her, if you like—I'm sure Hugo will be only too willing to hand her over!'

To Tammy's amazement David took the ring and put it into his pocket. She had not thought he would, not for one moment. She knew he was annoyed and suspicious, but she had not really thought he would agree to putting an end to their engagement just like that.

It was a relief, but on the other hand it did nothing for her pride. She couldn't accept that it was just because of her being on this boat, it had to go deeper than that.

Perhaps he had already been having second thoughts when he postponed the wedding, only she had been too obtuse to see it. Perhaps her falling in love with Hugo was a blessing in disguise as far as he was concerned, for it meant that she was the one who was finishing their engagement, not he.

'Very well, Tamsin,' said David stiffly, 'if that's what you want.'

He was making it look as though it was all her fault. Tammy's temper flared. 'What *I* want? It's what you want, isn't it, what you were angling for the moment you set foot on this boat? Well, let me tell you something about Andrea before you get too involved. She's a gold-digger. She only likes men with pots of money. When she finds out that you work for someone else, that your assets aren't quite what she hoped for, she'll drop you like a red-hot brick. She only got engaged to Hugo for his money, there's no love lost between them, even though they like to pretend there is.'

David drew on his cigarette, leaning back lazily against the wall as he exhaled the smoke, looking at her coolly through the blue haze. He was in complete control of himself now, calm and collected, no sign of anger, as though he was pleased with the way things had turned out.

'You know something, Tamsin? You're acting like one very jealous person.'

The very fact that he had got over his temper and had accepted that their engagement was finished incensed Tammy even more. 'Of Andrea? Why should I be jealous of her? She's a bitch, and I happen to know that Hugo was going to ditch her anyway.'

David said, 'If he took you into his confidence sufficiently to tell you that, I don't think I'm far wrong when I say there's something going on between you.'

Beyond caring now, Tammy cried, 'If you must know, I do love him!' She glared defiantly for a few moments before her face crumpled, all the fight gone out of her. Slow tears over which she had no control rolled down her cheeks. In a sad little voice she said, 'He doesn't love me, though, and as soon as I get my passport back I'm returning to London. I can't take much more, David.'

He moved towards her and without thinking she flung herself into his arms. 'Oh, David, David, what am I going to do?'

When Tammy thought about it later she realised it was ludicrous asking her ex-fiancé-of-one-minute for advice, but at that moment all she needed was comfort, the shelter of someone's arms, someone sympathetic, and surprisingly David was just that.

'Dear Tamsin,' he murmured, stroking her hair. 'You have got yourself into a pickle! If you really think there's no hope why don't you do what you should have done in the first place?'

'What's that?' she asked tearfully.

'Go to the police, report the loss of your belongings, and then go to the British Consulate. They're there to help you.'

'B-but Hugo said he'd help. He said he'd get my stuff back without having to bother with the formalities.' She didn't tell him that Hugo wouldn't let her off the boat, that he had kept her a virtual prisoner on the pretext that Emil Conin might draw her back into his lair once again. It made him sound detestable, and he wasn't that. Whatever motives he had for keeping her here she was sure they were perfectly honourable.

'Since he hasn't,' said David matter-of-factly, 'I think it's time you did something about it yourself. Unless you'd like me to?'

'I wish you would,' she cried at once. 'I want to go home. I can't tell you how much—and David, I'm sorry things haven't worked out between us. I think we both realise now that we weren't right for each other?'

He nodded and held her close. 'Yes, Tamsin, I'm sorry too, but I shall do all I can to help you. We're still friends, remember that. You can turn to me whenever you like.'

'Thanks,' she smiled weakly.

Suddenly the door burst roughly open. 'If you two lovers have finished,' Hugo's voice rasped into their silence, 'there's work waiting to be done, Miss Swift. It's time for lunch, in case you hadn't noticed.' His voice had never been more sarcastic.

Looking next at David, he continued, 'You're welcome to stay, but I'm afraid your fiancée won't be able to join you. But she does wait at table very charmingly.' The irony in his voice belied the compliment and Tammy turned her head away to hide the swift tears which were still all too near the surface. There was no need for that in front of David.

David squeezed her hand comfortingly. 'No, thanks, Kane, I'm off now. I have business to attend to,' and in an aside to Tammy, 'I'll be seeing you. Keep your pecker up!'

He left her then and Tammy followed, unable to bear the thought of being alone with Hugo in the mood he was in. She couldn't understand why he wasn't pleased that David had come to see her—unless of course he had found out about him and Andrea—and he was jealous, despite his avowal that he did not love the girl.

The meal was an uncomfortable affair, Tammy aware that both Hugo and Andrea were watching her closely, though probably for entirely different reasons.

Andrea to see whether she was jealous of her association with David, and Hugo—well, what was his interest? She didn't know, probably never would. He was an enigma, never for one moment allowing a third person to read his thoughts.

She did see him, though, staring at her ringless

left hand, and she was not surprised when he stayed behind after lunch. She had expected questions and had her answer prepared.

'What's happened?' he asked abruptly, as soon as they were alone.

She pretended not to know what he was talking about. 'What do you mean?'

'Between you and David Gordon,' he said tightly. 'It that why he came, to break off your engagement?'

Unconsciously she looked down at her hand, at the pale mark left on her finger, and hid it behind her back. 'No,' she said. 'As a matter of fact I finished it. He was two-timing me.'

Surprised brows rose. 'How do you know?'

'I saw him in Corsica—with Andrea.'

She felt tremendous satisfaction when she saw the shock her words gave him, but his voice gave away none of his feelings. 'Is that who it was? I saw someone run away, but I had no idea that——' He stopped and suddenly laughed.

'I don't think it's funny,' snapped Tammy.

'I do,' he said, his shoulders shaking with mirth. 'David and Andrea—it's too funny for words!'

'I'm glad you see it that way,' she said tightly, and so long as he did, so long as he did not realise that the real reason she had broken her engagement was because of her love for him, then that was all that mattered.

'But what was he doing in Corsica?' asked Hugo at length. 'I thought you said he was in New Zealand?'

'He was supposed to be,' she said tightly, pretending an anger she did not feel. 'He reckons he had some more business to attend to. It was news to me.'

'And do you mind?' he asked, his voice suddenly soft.

'There's not much point, is there? It won't alter things.' It wouldn't change the fact that Hugo did not love her, and that was what she desired most in the whole wide world.

She looked at him, seeing the lean, powerful strength of his body, the black hair and those smouldering dark sensual eyes, finely moulded lips that had once touched her own, and her heart cried. 'He's going to help me get back to London, Hugo. He's going to the police for me.'

He frowned blackly and savagely. 'That's ridiculous—we both know who stole your passport. It's not lost in the ordinary sense of the word.'

She shrugged. 'Perhaps the police will go and see Emil Conin. I don't know, all I know is that I want to get off this boat as soon as I can, and you're not helping.'

His lips thinned until they almost disappeared. 'I had hoped that you'd learn to enjoy life here. Seems I was mistaken.' He swung out without another word.

Was he annoyed because she had enlisted David's help, or because she had confessed to a wish to leave the *Flying Queen*? She would never understand him, never.

For the rest of the day Tammy was busy. She had all the morning's work to catch up on and she had no further time to dwell on either David's appearance or Hugo's attitude. She did notice, though, that Hugo had disappeared. He was not on the ship anywhere.

Had he, she mused, been spurred into trying to

find Emil Conin? Or was it some other business, not connected with her, that had taken him away? Funny he had not mentioned it that morning, in fact he had suggested they spend the day together. It must be that David's turning up had something to do with it.

Without realising it she waited restlessly for his return, carrying on with her work but with all her instincts alert.

When he did come back he sought her out immediately, taking her into his stateroom and pushing her down on to a hard, uncomfortable chair. 'I've seen David,' he said without preamble. 'We had a good long talk and he's said he'll leave everything to me.'

Tammy's heart stopped beating. David hadn't said anything about—no, he wouldn't. He was gentleman enough to respect her confidence—she hoped. When her heart began again it pumped so fiercely and drummed so loudly in her ears that she was sure he must hear it.

'What made him change his mind?' she asked breathlessly.

'I changed it for him,' said Hugo tersely. 'There's really no need for him to involve himself. Conin's a nasty piece of work, as you well know.'

'He wouldn't have had to see Conin,' she defended. 'The police would have done that. Had he been to see them when you saw him?'

He smiled drily. 'I met him outside. He was surprised to see me, but we had quite an illuminating talk. He said he was disappointed that things hadn't worked out between you, but that perhaps it was as well under the circumstances.'

'What circumstances?' she asked tentatively.

'Well, apparently he'd realised that he didn't love you enough to marry you, in fact he said he has no intention of getting married for several years yet. He wants to further his career.'

'He said that?' asked Tammy, shocked. 'He never told me, he led me to believe that——'

'He fancied Andrea? Perhaps he does, she's not an unattractive little thing. Perhaps he thought it an easy way out, especially as you showed yourself to be jealous of her.'

Tammy breathed easier. Good old David! She had been afraid to hear he had let her down, but instead he himself had taken the blame.

Hugo's voice softened now as he asked, 'Are you very upset?'

Tammy felt her breath catch in her throat. She wished he wouldn't look at her with so much concern, not if he didn't mean it. She shrugged indifferently. 'There are plenty more fish in the sea. I'm in no rush to get married.' In fact she doubted that she ever would. Hugo was the man she wanted. Hugo the unattainable. She pushed herself to her feet. 'If there's nothing else, can I go?'

Quite how she managed it Tammy did not know, but somehow she caught her heel in the leg of the chair. Hugo was there in a flash, arms outstretched, catching her before she pitched forward on to the floor.

He did not let her go immediately, but nor did he kiss her as Tammy had thought he might. Instead he looked down at her face, a peculiar expression in his handsome dark eyes, as though trying to understand her but failing.

Tammy's reaction to his nearness was electrifying. Never before had she felt such intense emotion, such pagan desire. For days her feelings had been bottled up, and it was as though his touch had released a trigger and it was all she could do to stop herself raising her lips to his, arching her body closer, to beg him to love her, as she loved him.

It could have been no more than five seconds that they stood there gazing into each other's eyes, but to Tammy it seemed an eternity, and when at length, with a harsh exclamation, he thrust her from him, her feelings exploded into frustrated rage.

But Hugo did not wait to see what effect his denial of her had. He strode from the room, the door banging behind him, adding emphasis to his departure.

Tammy collapsed in a heap on the floor and let the tears flow.

CHAPTER ELEVEN

TAMMY came to the conclusion, lying in bed that night, that there was no hope for her at all so far as Hugo was concerned. He had had the chance to make love to her—it must surely have been clear in her eyes—and spurned it. He had told her as clearly as if he had spoken that he had no physical interest in her whatsoever.

She wished with all her heart that she hadn't told him about David going to see about her passport.

Things might have been moving by now. As it was she was compelled to await his pleasure, right back to square one. 'Oh, damn, damn, damn!' she said expressively to the four walls of her cabin. 'Damn Hugo, damn David and damn Emil Conin!'

Two more days followed and still Tammy had no way of knowing whether Hugo was trying to recover her possessions. Sometimes he disappeared for several hours, but not once did he seek her out or give any indication that he had any news for her.

It was the end of her third week when Maggie Murray told her that their holiday was almost over. 'We fly back to Glasgow on Monday,' she said ruefully. 'We shall miss all this, we've had a wonderful time. And I shall miss you, Tammy. You mustn't forget to call in and see us if you're ever in our area.'

'I will,' said Tammy positively. 'How about the others, are they leaving too?'

'We're all going,' explained Maggie. 'The Andersons, of course, live in Monaco, so they haven't far to go, but Andrea and Hugo are returning to London. The *Flying Queen*'s being chartered by a group of Americans for the next three weeks. You should enjoy working for them, they're an ebullient crowd.'

Tammy said nothing, full of distress at the thought that she might be expected to stay on here indefinitely. 'Excuse me, Maggie,' she said suddenly, 'there's something I must do.'

Her lips were tight with anger as she knocked on Hugo's door. Without waiting for a reply she pushed her way inside, and as luck would have it he was alone. He looked surprised to see her, but smiled agreeably.

'I understand you're leaving here on Monday,' said Tammy sharply, and with no trace of an answering smile.

'That's right,' he said pleasantly. 'We're having a farewell party tomorrow night and for once I want you to forget your role and join us. I've hired someone else to do the waiting on.'

Tammy sniffed indifferently, wondering whether he was deliberately-being obtuse. She couldn't believe that he did not know why she had come to see him. 'I don't care about your party,' she said icily, 'what I want to know is what's happening to me? If you think I'm staying here after you've gone you're mistaken.'

He raised his brows mockingly. 'Doesn't the allure of the Mediterranean tempt you? Most girls I know would give up everything for a job like yours.'

'Then you won't have any difficulty in replacing me,' she returned coldly. 'Let me tell you this, Hugo Kane, if you haven't got my things here by the time you go on Monday, there'll be real trouble. I shan't only involve Emil Conin with the police, it will be you as well!'

His lips quirked. 'Darling Red, you never let me down. Did you honestly think I'd do that to you?'

'I wouldn't put anything past you,' she snapped. 'Have you been to see Emil Conin yet?'

He shrugged lazily, indifferently. 'Let's say you'll be flying with me on Monday and leave it at that.'

Tammy stared at him accusingly, her nostrils flared. '*You've got my passport!* You've had it ages, but you never told me. That's why you went after David. Damn you, Hugo! Why?'

'Because I enjoyed having you around,' he said

with a self-satisfied smile, no hint of apology in those handsome dark eyes.

'And you kept me here—you let me believe that——' She turned away angrily, disgustedly. 'I hate you, Hugo! I don't know what your motives are, and right at this moment I don't care, all I know is that I shall be glad when Monday comes and I won't have to see you again!'

She walked tiredly towards the door. Soon it would be all over, Hugo would be out of her life for ever—and it wasn't what she wanted, it wasn't. But she mustn't let him know this, not by the slightest flicker of an eyelash must she reveal her innermost thoughts.

'I was hoping you'd agree to see me in London.'

Hugo's voice reached her as she opened the door and she halted, turned, and looked at him dispiritedly. 'What for?' Her question was blunt to the point of rudeness, but this was the way it had to be. What point was there in being civil? What would it gain her?

He grinned. 'I enjoy your company, Red,' deliberately using the nickname he knew irritated her.

'But I don't enjoy yours,' she snapped, 'therefore I don't see the point in continuing a relationship that's never got off the ground from the beginning.'

'We'd be equals in London,' he said. 'I wouldn't be your employer, it could make a difference.'

'I doubt it,' she said shortly. 'Nothing could ever make any difference to the way I feel about you.'

She closed the door before he could answer. It was the truth, though he would never know in what way, and she couldn't even begin to think why he should want to see her again. If she had thought there might be some future in it, a slight hope that he might return her feelings, then she might have agreed. But knowing Hugo as she did, knowing the sort of man he was, she could only assume that the offer had been made out of kindness, though goodness knows she wasn't aware that he had a kind streak in him. Perhaps his conscience was bothering him, perhaps he finally regretted the way he had treated her and saw this as a sort of peace offering? She snorted derisively and went to her own cabin.

After lunch the next day Tammy found that her time was her own. The hired help had arrived and she was left with nothing to do but get ready for the evening.

It was a novelty, this life of leisure, and she took a long bath before lying down on her bed with a book. She could have gone up on to the sun deck, but somehow she did not want to force herself into small talk. Maggie was all right on her own, but with Penny and Andrea present, she knew the afternoon would be anything but relaxed.

The evening would be bad enough; Andrea would still look upon her as an employee of Hugo's no matter what he said to the contrary, and would more than likely go out of her way to make the evening as unpleasant as possible. On top of that she would be the odd one out, so it would be uncomfortable anyway.

It was after eight and still Tammy had not left her room. Thoughts of the unpleasantness that could lie ahead made her reluctant to join the others, and it was not until a knock came on her door that she dragged herself to her feet.

She expected it to be Hugo, demanding to know

why she hadn't yet put in an appearance, and was stunned to see David. 'You—what are you doing here?'

He grinned easily. 'Special invitation by the man himself. Come on up, everyone's wondering where you are.'

She took his arm gladly, feeling easier now that she had an escort. But once up on the sun deck where the others were enjoying drinks and dancing to music relayed over the whole ship, he was claimed by Andrea and when she next saw him they were dancing cheek to cheek.

She sat on one of the cushioned seats, a glass of Pernod in her hand, watching them miserably. She wasn't jealous, it was the fact that she felt so alone. Penny was with her husband, and Maggie with hers, and now that Andrea had claimed David it only left Hugo, and he was nowhere in sight. Not that she wanted his company; having to make light conversation with him would be as bad as being left on her own.

But when suddenly she felt someone sit down beside her she knew it was him without even looking. The hairs down her spine prickled and she tensed herself for the inevitable battle.

'Why did you invite David?' she asked abruptly, turning her head and catching her breath at the sight of him in a cream evening jacket. It emphasised the depth of his tan, brought into sharp relief the gleaming black hair which had been tamed tonight so that it lay sleekly about his well-shaped head.

His lips quirked. 'You wouldn't believe me if I told you, so let's say it was because Andrea suggested it. I hope their being together won't cause you too much distress.'

Tammy tightened her lips, finding it easy to pretend that she was jealous of the other girl. 'I'll try not to let it bother me,' and she let her eyes seek out the other couple as though she found it hard to ignore the man she was supposed to love.

Hugo's hand covered hers, turning her startled gaze to him. 'Don't let them upset you,' he said softly, with concern on his face she found hard to believe was genuine. 'Let's dance,' and he pulled her gently up and drew her into his arms.

The music was a soft, dreamy waltz and their two bodies merged into one, drifting in the shadows of the muted coloured lights which had been strung about the deck. Tammy felt unbelievably happy. She pushed to the back of her mind the thought that Hugo was only being nice to her because he thought her envious of Andrea. Tonight was hers, a memory to be treasured when she went back to London, when Hugo was gone out of her life for ever.

Unconsciously she moved in his arms, holding herself closer to his hard maleness, closing her eyes so that she could forget everyone else and take all this moment had to offer. For a few hours, she would pretend that Hugo loved her.

A meal followed later and then it was back on deck for dancing again. It was a clear, still night, warm, with a pendulous moon, a perfect setting for romance.

Andrea had not left David's side all evening and he was making an excellent job of pretending to be the devoted lover. In fact, if Hugo had not told her otherwise, Tammy would have thought that

David really was keen on the dark girl. Andrea
would be in for a big disappointment when she discovered that he was only amusing himself at her
expense. Tammy felt sorry for her in one respect,
but she had only to remind herself of the way she
had chased after Hugo, wanting him only for his
material wealth, for the feeling to vanish.

Despite the fact that Hugo danced with her all
evening he made no attempt to kiss her, not even
show by the pressure of his hands that he found her
attractive. He was doing his duty, Tammy thought
bitterly. He was keeping her happy because David
had fallen in love with another girl.

It mattered not to him that Andrea had changed
her affections; most probably it was a relief. It
would save him the job of having to let her down
later. But he need not have made it so patently obvious that he was only doing what he thought right
under the circumstances.

Perhaps some of her resentment showed on her
face, Tammy didn't know, but when the evening
ended, when the music stopped and it was time to go
to bed, Hugo said, 'I want a word with you.'

She shrugged and followed him to his stateroom,
wondering why what he wanted to say couldn't have
been said during the course of the evening. But she
was too tired to worry about it much and as soon as
she was inside she collapsed on to a chair and kicked
off her shoes.

- 'Have you enjoyed this evening?' he asked, re-
moving his jacket and punctiliously hanging it up
inside his wardrobe. Next he took off his bow tie
and undid the front of his shirt, revealing the power-

ful muscular chest with its covering of fine dark hairs.

Despite her animosity Tammy could not help harbouring a desire to run her fingers across his chest, to feel for herself the latent strength of his body, and so great was her urge that it took a tremendous effort to drag her eyes up to his face.

He was watching her, smiling enigmatically. 'Well, have you?'

She had almost forgotten he had spoken. Now she nodded emphatically. 'It's been marvellous. Quite the best night I've spent on the *Flying Queen*.'

'Then why,' he was frowning now, 'did I detect a trace of bitterness in your attitude towards the end of the evening?'

'You know how I feel about David,' she prevaricated, shocked that he had so easily read her mind. 'I appreciate your trying to help, and to a certain extent it worked, but——'

'But nothing,' he cut in hotly. 'Your animosity was directed at me. Do you really hate me so much that even on your last night you cannot hide your feelings?'

She could have wept. Couldn't he see that it was love that was driving her crazy, not hatred? Didn't he know that her heart was breaking into tiny pieces and that each time he touched her it was sweet torment, that she hungered for more than the conventional politeness he had shown?

From somewhere she managed to drag up enough strength to say calmly, 'I'm sorry if that's the impression I gave—it wasn't intentional, I assure you.'

'Then what was it?' he demanded angrily. 'Surely it wouldn't have been too much of a hardship to hide your feelings for a few hours? I almost wish I hadn't invited David.'

'Then why did you?' asked Tammy heatedly, 'when you know how I'd react seeing him and Andrea together?' Somehow she had to go on with this charade of being the injured party.

'As a matter of fact,' he said coolly, 'I wanted to see for myself whether it was true that you really were jealous, or whether it was some tale David had concocted for my benefit.'

She regarded him haughtily. 'And what conclusion did you reach?'

Hugo looked at her intently for a few minutes and Tammy felt the colour rise in her cheeks, but she stared back defiantly and waited for his answer.

His face an impassive mask, he replied slowly, 'I decided that you didn't love him after all and that you couldn't give two hoots about him drooling over Andrea.'

Tammy's resolve that he shouldn't learn the truth from her stiffened and she stood up, slipping her feet back into her shoes. 'That's where you're wrong, Mr Kane. I care very much about David and it hurt me dreadfully to see him with Andrea.' There was even a break in her voice, adding conviction to her words. The truth of the matter was that she felt like sobbing—for a love that could never be. 'If you've quite finished with me,' she continued, 'I'd like to go to bed. It's been a long evening.'

She could see the effort it cost him to control an angry reply and as he walked stiffly towards the door she felt like throwing herself at him, declaring that it had all been lies and that her love for David had died a natural death the day she met him.

But the door was open, her opportunity gone. With her chin tilted high Tammy stalked past him along the carpeted corridor and down the stairs to her own room.

That was it, she thought. The end. Tomorrow they would each go their different ways and she would never see him again.

She undressed and slid into bed, knowing that she would not sleep despite the fact that she was desperately tired. When a tap sounded on her door she buried her head beneath the sheets and refused to answer. Damn the man! Couldn't he give her any peace?

When she heard the door open Tammy knew she should have guessed he would not go away until he had settled whatever it was he had come for, so slowly she dragged the sheets from her face, only to find that it was David who confronted her and not the man she had dreaded to see.

'What do *you* want?' she asked rudely, her row with Hugo still rankling.

David sat down on the edge of the bed. 'What's up?' he asked kindly. 'I thought I'd find you radiating happiness.

'What have I got to be happy about?' she demanded crossly.

'Was I mistaken, then?' he frowned. 'Weren't you and Hugo getting on as well as it appeared?'

Tammy pulled herself up. 'We weren't getting on at all,' she snapped. 'He's a bore and I hate him.'

David looked surprised and then grinned. 'Oh, I see, a lovers' tiff. Never mind, Tamsin, you know what they say, the course of true love never did run smooth.'

'Love!' she scoffed, her beautiful green eyes moist with unshed, angry tears. 'Where does love come into it? Hugo doesn't love me.'

'What makes you so sure?' His voice was oddly changed. 'You looked happy enough together.'

'He was doing me a favour,' she said sarcastically. 'Trying to keep me cheerful because you were patronising Andrea. Why did you tell him that I was jealous of her?'

He shrugged. 'I thought it might help. I'm sorry, Tamsin, if I've messed things up, but when he told me he loved you I was under the impression that it would only be a matter of time before you two got together permanently. Hugo struck me as being the type of man who always gets what he wants, and as I knew you loved him, I thought it might add spice to your relationship if he thought you still loved me. I thought he would go all out to get you since he knew that our engagement was over.'

Tammy was hardly listening. 'David!' she cried eagerly, incredulously. 'Did I hear you right? Hugo —loves—me?' Hope tempered her voice and coloured her cheeks. 'Did he really say that?'

David nodded. 'That's why I thought, when I saw you together, that——'

But he got no further. Tammy was out of bed and flying across the room. 'Sorry, David, there are some things that can't wait!'

But outside Hugo's room she hesitated, asking herself whether she was doing the right thing. If Hugo did love her wouldn't he do the chasing? Wouldn't he have made some attempt to win her away from David?

She had in fact seen less of him since that day

David had flown in than she had before. If he did love her then he had a strange way of showing it, and she was not so sure that she was brave enough to jump in with both feet on the chance that she might be rebuffed.

So, her feet dragging, she went back to her room. David had disappeared and she climbed into bed for the second time that night, eventually falling into a fitful sleep.

Monday morning stole upon them with leaden skys. The weather forecast promised much-needed rain and Tammy felt more miserable than ever before.

She showered and dressed, then stood for a few moments looking at her new clothes in the wardrobe. They would have to stay; she wanted no memories of this holiday, nothing at all that would remind her of the man who had bought them, whom, after today, she must thrust irrevocably from her mind.

The thought that he might conceivably love her had tormented her all night long, and there were dark shadows beneath her eyes as she made her way up to the main deck.

Chips had the inevitable pot of coffee ready and waiting and poured her a cup when she entered the kitchen. 'Your late night's telling on you,' he said lightly, but not unkindly. 'Pity your flight's so early or you could have had an extra hour.'

'I'd rather be home,' said Tammy tiredly.

'With weather like this I don't blame you, but I don't expect you'll find it any better in London, not if I know the English weather.'

'I don't mind,' said Tammy. 'I've had about as

much as I can take and I'm looking forward to the peace and quiet of my flat.'

Chips seemed in the mood for conversation this morning and Tammy wished he would shut up. Even so she couldn't rebuff him, he was far too nice for that. But when he said, 'I'm sorry to hear that you and your boy-friend have split up,' she almost wished she had told him.

'I gather it was Andrea's doing?' he continued. 'But still, he wasn't much of a man if he could do that to you, was he?'

Tammy said vehemently, 'I've finished with men altogether, Chips. They're not worth bothering with, none of them,' and she broke down into the tears which should have come last night but didn't.

He looked embarrassed and uncomfortable, but it was not until Hugo spoke behind her back that she realised why.

'A fit of the tantrums, Miss Swift? I thought you'd be overjoyed at going.'

'Oh, I am, I am,' she sobbed angrily, 'glad to get rid of the whole lot of you!' She refused to look at him, his harsh tones had told her what sort of mood he was in.

When he caught her arm she pulled crossly away.

'I had a visitor this morning,' he said quietly.

Tammy held her breath. He was going to say it was David! She knew he was. Wait till she saw him —she would *kill* him!

'And we had a very interesting discussion. Seems like you were going to come and see me last night. What made you change your mind?'

She stared stubbornly at the wall, aware that both Chips and Hugo were awaiting her reply. She could imagine the chef's mouth open with curiosity, and Hugo—well, he wanted an answer, but he had not sounded as though it bothered him very much.

'Isn't it a woman's prerogative?' she asked woodenly.

'Without a doubt,' acknowledged Hugo, 'but there's usually a reason.' He clamped his hand on her shoulder, making her wince. 'I suggest we go along to my room and talk it over.'

'There's nothing to say,' she insisted, still refusing to turn and look at him, afraid that once she saw that beloved face she might break down and confess her love.

But Hugo swung her round, saying harshly, 'I beg to differ. I think we have a whole lot to say to each other. We can talk here, if you like, in front of Chips. I'm sure he won't mind, in fact he might find it highly entertaining.'

Tammy's eyes flickered towards the cook, whose face was alight with interest, and she managed a weak apologetic smile. 'I don't seem to have any choice, Mr Kane,' she said slowly, allowing him to propel her towards the door, all the time conscious of his touch and the shock waves going through her system.

In his cabin he sat her forcibly down on a chair and stood in front of her, his feet apart and his hands clasped behind his back. 'Now,' he said sternly, 'what was it you were going to come and tell me last night?'

Tammy bit her lower lip and remained silent, staring straight ahead at a shirt button, noting inconsequentially how it moved with the regularity of his breathing.

'Tammy!' his voice even more harsh, 'I want an answer—*now*.' When she still made no attempt to speak he lifted her chin, compelling her to look at him.

She tried to return his gaze with a calmness she was far from feeling, but failed miserably when she felt her love welling up inside, and she averted her eyes, clamping her lips together obstinately.

If he would only say that he loved her how easy it would be, but like this, when his face was a hard, implacable mask, how could she? What if David had been wrong and Hugo didn't love her? He certainly didn't look as though he did, anyone less lover-like would be hard to find.

His fingers tightened on her chin and Tammy felt tears springing to her eyes, but whether they were tears of pain or because of the unfortunate situation in which she now found herself she was not sure. But when they rolled down her cheeks and across the strong brown fingers, Hugo drew in his breath harshly and pulled her roughly up into his arms.

'Tammy, tell me, damn you, tell me!' he rasped, holding her against him.

When Tammy felt his vibrant strength flow into her it broke down the last of her defences and she moulded herself against the iron-hard body, crying openly now. What did it matter if he didn't love her? She would never know any peace until she told him. 'I love you,' she whispered into his shoulder.

He tensed and held her from him. 'What did you say?' and he sounded incredulous, as though he thought he was hearing things.

Tammy's hopes were dashed. She was quite sure

he had heard and was making her say it again to embarrass her. It meant nothing to him, it couldn't do. 'I love you,' she repeated miserably, still not lifting her head.

'Look at me and say it,' he ordered sternly.

Tammy's head felt like a ton weight as she raised it until her eyes met his, hard dark ones with no hint of emotion. His coolness irritated her, bringing her weak body back to life. 'I love you,' she cried loudly, 'do you hear, Hugo Kane, I love you! Go on, laugh yourself silly now I've admitted it. Tell me I'm a fool, but I can't help it, it's something over which I have no control. But you needn't worry that I shall make a nuisance of myself, once I'm back in England you'll never see me again.'

Completely spent now, she sagged against him, allowing herself one last glorious moment of feeling his magnificent body next to hers. It was strange, she thought, that his heart should beat as rapidly as hers. Was he really so annoyed about her confession?

'I love you too, Tammy.'

His voice seemed to reach her from a distance and she stilled, listening and waiting, wondering whether he would repeat those magic words—or had it all been a figment of her imagination? Something she had dreamed of for so long that she had willed herself into hearing words that were never said.

But when he tilted her chin and looked down into her eyes he did not have to speak for her to see the love reflected there.

'Oh, Hugo!' and she lifted her mouth to meet his, ready with a warm, hungry response.

Time stood still. Never before had a kiss meant so much. It was the answer to all her prayers, it was

Hugo's declaration of love, it meant everything and told her everything. She rose to heights never before experienced. His mouth possessed her, ravaged her senses until her bones melted and she belonged to him for all time.

How long it was before he let her go Tammy never knew. It was eternity, yet only a few seconds. It was a lifetime in one short minute. Her breathing was rapid and her trembling limbs so weak that had he not led her over to the bed she would have fallen.

They sat down side by side on the edge, his arm firmly clamped about her waist. 'Darling Tammy,' he said hoarsely, 'I never thought I'd hear you say it. Just think, if David hadn't told me I'd have let you go today and we might never have seen each other again. I don't think I could have stood it.'

'You gave no inkling.' Her eyes glazed painfully. 'I had no idea you felt as you did. You hid it perfectly—why?'

He grimaced wryly. 'You loved David—or so you kept telling me. It was not until I saw the two of you together that I realised you didn't love him at all. But even then I never dreamt it was because of me. You'd always vowed hatred.'

'Self-defence,' admitted Tammy. 'Was that why you never told me that you'd got my things back off Emil Conin?'

He nodded. 'I wanted to keep you here as long as possible, but it was becoming more and more difficult to convince you that I was trying to help. It hurt me to hurt you, do you know that, and when you told me that you'd enlisted David's help I had to act quickly. I took a risk when I told him I loved you, but it worked—and we have only David to thank now that we've discovered how we really feel about each other.'

They kissed again and Tammy snuggled contentedly against him. 'I'm sorry about Eddie. I didn't really like him, I only did it out of contrariness because you'd warned me about him.'

'I know now,' he said, his lips suddenly grim. 'But that time he nearly raped you I could have killed him—you too, come to that, I thought you were a willing partner. But even so, even if I did rate you as immoral I still couldn't help loving you—and that time you and he were late coming back I was out of my mind with worry.'

'How do you think I felt?' she asked drily. 'I was terrified, and when you told me afterwards that there might have been bandits lurking, I nearly died!'

He laughed suddenly. 'I'm afraid I was pulling your leg—there are no bandits these days. But at least it had the desired effect. I haven't seen you with Eddie since.'

'As a matter of fact,' she said self-consciously, 'I think it's because I told him I loved you.'

Hugo looked astonished. 'You knew then?'

'I think I loved you the first moment I saw you, only I wasn't aware of it. You were different from any other man I'd met, and you certainly made me forget David. I hardly thought of him those first days here.'

'And now, have you any regrets?' He put the question softly, his arm warm and comforting about her, as though he was never going to let her go.

She shook her head, her emerald eyes alight with adoration. 'I don't think so, not about David anyway, but are *you* sure? Do you remember that time when you said you wished you'd never set eyes on me? You were so cruel. And then, here in this very room, I nearly fell and you caught me—remember? I desperately wanted you to kiss me, but you didn't —you pushed me away as if you couldn't stand the sight of me. Why?'

'Tammy, my God, you don't know how hard it was for me to resist. Your eyes were pleading with me and I knew that in that moment I could have taken you, but I thought it was because of David and Andrea—and I didn't want you on the re-bound, not at any cost.'

'There's no fear of that,' she smiled. 'I love you with every fibre of my being.'

'Me too, Tammy, but there is one more thing I want to put straight.'

She raised her fine brows. 'I can't think of any-thing else that bothers me.'

'You once said,' he explained patiently, 'that you detested the type of person I am. What was it you called me—one of the idle rich?'

Tammy coloured delicately. 'I'm sorry. I've real-ised now that it doesn't matter. I suppose you earn your money somehow, but it's not your wealth I'm interested in, it's you.'

'I'm grateful to hear it,' he mocked lightly, 'but to put you in the picture before you become Mrs Hugo Kane I think I ought to tell you that I have a very flourishing business and I take a very active part in it myself.' He paused before continuing, 'Aren't you going to ask me what it is? Shipbuilding. High class luxury yachts—I design them. The *Flying Queen* is my favourite.'

But Tammy wasn't listening. Mrs Hugo Kane—didn't it sound wonderful? She looked at her pirate lover with stars in her eyes, patting his cheek playfully. 'I've told you, I don't care what you do. The less time you spend at work the more you can spend with me—and that's where I want you—right by my side, for the rest of my life.'

'Darling, darling Red, I still can't believe it.'

Tammy's eyes flashed attractively. 'Let's get one thing straight, Hugo—my hair is not red, it's auburn.'

He grinned impishly. 'To me it's red, and it's the part about you I love best, the part that attracted me to you in the first place. That and your adorable temper.'

Before Tammy could protest Hugo's mouth was on hers, his lips tantalisingly sensual, making her forget her cross words and give herself up to the man she loved heart and soul.

When he pushed her away abruptly she was surprised, wondering what other obstacle he was going to put in their path.

But he was grinning. 'Much as I hate to let you go, we do have a plane to catch.'

Tammy lay back provocatively. 'I don't care. I feel I could stay here for the rest of my life.'

'You've changed your tune,' he joked, 'but don't forget, there's a whole crowd of Americans coming tomorrow, and I certainly don't intend risking you to one of them.'

She laughed. 'You won't, not ever, to anyone. But promise me one thing, Hugo, let's come back here for our honeymoon.'

His eyes twinkled. 'Anything you say, Red, anything at all.' He ducked as her arm came flying towards his face, catching it and carrying her hand to his lips. 'My delightful little hothead, how I love you!'

And she replied, 'And my gorgeous, cruel pirate, how *I* love *you*.'